The *1895* Murder

A Sebastian McCabe – Jeff Cody Mystery

Dan Andriacco

Dan Andriacco

Paperback ISBN 9781780922379
ePub ISBN 9781780922386
PDF ISBN 9781780922393

Published in the UK by MX Publishing
335 Princess Park Manor, Royal Drive,
London, N11 3GX
www.mxpublishing.com
Cover design by www.staunch.com

This book is lovingly dedicated to our guys

DAN, MIKE, AND BETH

CONTENTS

But there can be no grave for Sherlock Holmes or Doctor Watson . . . Shall they not always live in Baker Street? Are they not there this moment, as one writes? . . . Outside, the hansoms rattle through the rain and Moriarty plans his latest deviltry. Within, the sea coal flames upon the hearth and Holmes and Watson take their well-won ease. So they still live for all that love them well: in a romantic chamber of the heart, in a nostalgic country of the mind, where it is always 1895.

Vincent Starrett,
The Private Life of Sherlock Holmes

Dan Andriacco

Chapter One
Overture

Opening night of Sebastian McCabe's first play went off without a hitch, except for the dead body—the off-stage one. For me, the murder hit close to home and distracted me from the chaos surrounding my upcoming wedding. That was the upside.

The downside was that, not for the first time in my association with Mac, I almost got killed. I don't blame the play for that, but it's hard to separate the two events in my mind.

My brother-in-law has written half a dozen mystery novels about his amateur sleuth, a magician named Damon Devlin. But he probably never would have felt the need to write a play if Lafcadio Figg hadn't moved to Erin.

Mac and Figg had known each other for years as members of the Anglo-Indian Club, a scion society of the Baker Street Irregulars in Cincinnati, about 40 miles downriver from our little town. Since I've never been to one of their meetings, I have no idea how the club managed to fit both egos into one room. It must have been quite a trick.

Figg is a retired high school drama teacher whose mannerisms tend toward the dramatic. A short, stocky fellow with gray chin-length hair and mutton-chop whiskers, he looks like somebody out of another century. At times he even wears a cape. I keep expecting him to say "Egad!" or maybe even "Gadzooks!" But there's no denying his energy. He hadn't been in Erin more than a month before he hatched the idea of acquiring the abandoned Odd Fellows Hall on Broadway Street and turning it into a theater. By the end of his first year in town he had patched together enough money from donations and grants to make it happen.

From the start, Mac was outwardly enthusiastic about the project. I couldn't help but wonder, though, how long he was going to let the new kid on the block have the spotlight to himself. The answer came one winter evening when I had walked next door from my carriage house apartment to shoot the breeze in Mac's study before going out to dinner with my fiancée, Lynda Teal.

After circling for a while around the subject of the new theater, which would be called the Lyceum, Mac finally came out with his news:

"A new theater deserves a new play, Jefferson, and I am just the person to write it. For a strong start to this noble venture, the drama should be one with instant audience appeal. I was thinking, perhaps, of a Sherlock Holmes adventure."

"Of course you were." I sighed. With Figg and Mac both involved, how could it be anything else? It was a cinch they weren't going to ask me to adapt one of my unpublished Max Cutter mystery novels. "Are you sure you can work with Figg?"

"And why the devil not, old boy? Are we not both mature individuals?"

I wasn't sure either of them was, but I let that pass. "You realize, of course, that you can't play Sherlock Holmes."

Okay, I admit that was a little cruel. Mac is by nature a performer, like every great teacher. He'd even been a professional magician in Europe as a young man. But the only way he could ever portray Sherlock Holmes would be on the radio or in some other kind of audio production. He carries something close to a hundred pounds more than he should on his five-ten frame and he wears a full beard.

"Perhaps not," he conceded with a "gotcha" smile. "However, my girth would certainly be no bar to assuming the role of Mycroft Holmes, old boy."

He had me there. I'm no Sherlockian, but even I know that Mycroft is Sherlock's smarter and wider brother. The plan was clear now: Mac would write a script giving Mycroft the best lines. Oh, Figg was going to love this.

"You'd have to shave off your beard," I pointed out, enjoying the role of spoilsport. The ill-fated Peter Gerard may have played Sherlock Holmes with a goatee in his controversial movie *221B Bourbon Street*, but Sherlockians were still screaming about that even though Gerard was dead.

Mac struck a noble pose. "Like all true artists, I am willing to sacrifice for my art."

So that's how the play came about. Looking for a Holmes story to dramatize, Mac turned to one of the two in which Mycroft had a speaking part. It's called "The Adventure of the Bruce-Partington Plans," but Mac named the play based on it *1895*. That's the year in which the story takes place. Apparently it also has great symbolic value to Sherlockians as a magic year or something. Mac even brandishes those four digits on the rear end of his 1959 Chevy in the form of an oval bumper sticker—right next to his 221B license plate.

In the next few months, Mac was a tornado of activity instead of a mere whirlwind. In addition to finishing his yearly mystery novel and keeping up his day job as a professor and head of the popular culture program at St. Benignus College, he managed to write the play, land the role as Mycroft (Figg made him audition), and become a founding member of the Lyceum Players.

And he wasn't the only McCabe involved in this project. My sister, the artist Kathleen Cody McCabe, designed her husband a cool poster that started appearing around town in early April. At the top in bold was the name of the play: **1895**. Beneath, in the center of the poster, were two silhouettes like a pair of unmatched bookends. The unmistakable outline of Sherlock Holmes looked off to the right and a more corpulent form faced left. The words on the left said:

Plans stolen . . .

an official killed . . .
And on the right:
M needs
the help of one man,
his brother—
The sentence was completed at the bottom:
Sherlock Holmes

All of this was barely on my radar screen, though, because I was involved in another highly complicated theatrical production—the wedding of Lynda Teal and Thomas Jefferson Cody. After four years of serious dating, a little over four weeks of estrangement, six months of limbo, and an engagement of about eight months, we were scheduled to walk down the aisle at St. Edward the Confessor Catholic Church on Saturday, May 26. That was the weekend after *1895* completed its two-weekend run.

In the several months leading up to that happy day I helped Lynda plan the wedding. This consisted mostly of saying, "Great idea!" Admittedly, that wasn't so tough. But the whole planning thing had gotten a lot more stressful recently with Lynda's parents coming to town. (You'll see what I mean later.) So, by the time *1895* opened, I was ready for a relaxing evening at the theater.

Yeah, well, that didn't work out so great for Abraham Lincoln, either.

Chapter Two
A Killer Opening

From the opening night excitement, you would have thought we were on Broadway, New York, not Broadway Street, Erin, Ohio. Never mind that most of the actors were ordinary folks that we knew in real life, amateurs who had never trod the boards before. This was *opening night* at the Lyceum.

Lynda was dressed in a bright yellow dress, close to the color of her Mustang, but much more frilly and feminine than the muscle car. It had a boat neck, poufy short sleeves, and a hem that fell just above her sandals. She wore her curly, honey-blond hair in a French braid, showing off a pair of simple gold earrings that contrasted well with her dark complexion. She looked like a million neatly bundled euros, and was just as stacked. I smiled.

"You look happy," she said in her husky voice.

"I'm looking at you."

"Well, look a little higher, will you?"

Methinks the lady didst protest too much. I was pretty sure she wasn't working out with me in the gym every day because she didn't want anybody to notice her curvaceous figure. But I did as requested and refocused on her oval face and gold-flecked eyes. That wasn't a bad view, either. I leaned forward.

"Nice crowd," Lynda said, pointedly ignoring my body language.

If she was trying to get me to take my eyes off of her, it worked. I looked around the newly renovated hall. The house was packed, and many of the faces familiar. One of the first I noticed was "Father Joe" Pirelli, the long-tenured and much-loved president of St. Benignus College, where Mac and I both labor. Although the smiling, white-haired priest is everybody's best friend, he seems to have a special weakness for Mac, a former student of his. The college was also represented by numerous professors, Tony Lampwicke of campus radio station WIJC, and my administrative assistant, Aneliese Pokorny.

I was just waving at our honorable mayor, the elegant Lesley Saylor Mackie, when Henry Wilcox made his entrance. Drama critics don't just show up; they make entrances. In his case he moved slowly, further enhancing my impression that his rounded shoulders, bald head and hooked nose make him look rather like a turtle.

"The working press has arrived," I said to Lynda *sotto voce.*

"I've been here," she sniffed.

As former news editor of *The Erin Observer & News Ledger*, Lynda had once been Henry's boss, tasked with the considerable task of straightening out the freelance contributor's tangled sentence structure. Last fall she'd been bucked up the corporate ladder, to editorial director of Grier Ohio NewsGroup. I'd gotten quite a bit of mileage out of her removal from the trenches, implying with some frequency that Lynda was no longer a real journalist. I made a mental note that the joke had just about worn out its welcome.

"There's Polly's friend, Bill," I said, pointing rudely. He was a medium-sized guy, mid-thirties, with dark hair and a mustache.

"He looks military," said Lynda, who should know.

"That didn't take a Sherlock Holmes," I said. Everything about the guy looked military, including the haircut. Besides, Polly must have told Lynda that they'd met in the Army. Sister Mary Margaret Malone—Polly to Lynda, although

Triple M is my own private nickname for her—is Lynda's best friend, maid of honor at our wedding, and a religious sister (like a nun, but technically not exactly).

Just then the lights lowered and a voice that I recognized as belonging to Lafcadio Figg came booming over the loudspeaker:

"Ladies and gentlemen, the world premier performance of *1895* by Sebastian McCabe is about to begin. Please turn off your cell phones . . ." And so forth. I pulled out my iPhone and set it on vibrate. I guess some people actually turn off their phones occasionally, but as public relations director for St. Benignus, always on call, I don't have that luxury.

The first scene of *1895* is a kind of brief prologue acted out in near darkness before the drawn curtain, based on the end of "The Adventure of the Empty House." This is the story where Sherlock Holmes, long thought to be dead at the Reichenbach Falls, makes his dramatic reappearance. He captures Col. Sebastian Moran, Professor Moriarty's top henchman, in the act of shooting what turns out to be a wax bust of the detective displayed in the window of 221B Baker Street. The scene ends with Inspector Lestrade saying, "Good to see you back in London, sir."

Jonathan Hawes, of Hawes & Holder Funeral Home, made a convincing Sherlock Holmes, tall and lean. For weeks Lynda had nagged me—seriously or not, I could never tell—to audition for the part. I have the height, six-one, and I'm not a pound overweight. In my opinion even my red hair was no stumbling block—if there can be a blonde James Bond, why not a red-headed Sherlock Holmes? But I'm not the acting type. I've had enough drama in my life, thank you.

Caleb Wilson, owner of Auld Lang Syne Antiques & Collectibles, put on a mustache to become Dr. Watson. According to the program, he also provided a lot of the props to convincingly recreate the Holmes-Watson sitting room in the 221B Baker Street scenes of the play. Paul Rand, a retired IRS agent, was a suitably nasty Col. Sebastian Moran, and Lt. Col. L.

Jack Gibbons played Lestrade. I've known Gibbons, the police chief's best officer and now his assistant chief, for years. I never knew he had a first name, though, until I read the program. And I still didn't know what it was, unless it was "L."

The program, by the way, was a work of art all its own. Kate's poster was reproduced on the outside, losing none of its pizzazz by being reduced in size. Inside was an essay by Figg about the dramatic history of the hall, plus ads by every business or non-profit entity in town, from the giants— Gamble Bank & Trust Co., the Altiora Corp., St. Benignus College, you name it—down to the little storefronts downtown, like Garrison's Antiques. The listing of Lyceum board members on page five was like a "Who's Who" of local heavyweights, starting with board president Elijah Gamble. I guess he didn't have enough to do as chairman of the family bank.

The main action of the play gets underway when the curtain goes up on the sitting room in Baker Street with its authentically antique wingback chairs and love seat in front of the fireplace. Now it's the year following the events of the prologue. Cribbing dialogue straight from "The Adventure of the Bruce-Partington Plans," Holmes complains that with the removal of Moriarty and Moran, "the London criminal is a very dull fellow."

Sitting in the audience, I felt a strange mental dichotomy. On the one hand, I bought into the illusion in the same way that any theatergoer must. But at the same time, I was remembering what lay on the other side of the painted sets. Lynda and I had visited a few days ago, curious because we knew so many people that were involved in one way or another.

In the final week before the first production of a new theatrical troupe in a newly reconstituted theater, all was chaos. The set was in place, but not quite finished. Hammers were banging in the back even as actors were rehearsing in street clothes. Lafcadio Figg, his cape aflutter, was yelling at Mac, like

Napoleon barking orders at Waterloo. "No, no, no! You're supposed to be Mycroft Holmes, McCabe, not Nero Wolfe!" The poor man was under the illusion that he was actually the director of the play. Mac, freshly shorn of his beard for the first time since I'd known him in college, replied with a haughty, "And I suppose you would know the character better than the author of the drama, Lafcadio?"

Jonathan Hawes, Caleb Williams and Lt. L. Jack Gibbons smirked at that in synch, as if they'd been choreographed.

"Let's get out of here before somebody gets hurt," I told Lynda.

We went backstage, where things were noisier but less contentious. Some of the actors whose parts came later or earlier than the part being rehearsed were standing around. I immediately noticed Trixie LaBelle, who played the part of Miss Violet Westbury, fiancée of the murder victim, Arthur Cadogan West. In Mac's version, Dr. Watson offers his comfort to the bereaved woman and the final scene carries an implication that they will marry. I could understand that. Trixie looked quite fetching in her T-shirt and shorts, lustrous auburn hair hanging loose. I'd never seen her long legs before, and they were something to see. One of them was adorned with a bright red rose tattoo.

"Hi, Jeff!" she called. "How ya been?"

"Well, I haven't seen you lately. That's a good thing, no offense. This is my fiancée, Lynda Teal. Lynda, this Dr. Trixie LaBelle."

"Nice to meet you."

"Charmed," Lynda said. She didn't sound like she meant it. I didn't know what was wrong with her, but I had a feeling I would find out.

"Well, break a leg," I told Trixie. *No, don't do that! I like your legs just the way they are.*

"Oh, there's Polly," Lynda said.

We started toward her, Lynda hanging onto my arm possessively. I waved goodbye to Trixie, no doubt with a helpless look on my face.

"So what's Trixie a doctor of?" Lynda asked in low voice. "Pole dancing, maybe?"

"She's my urologist."

"What! You mean she . . . I mean, you—"

"I had a kidney stone last year. My regular doctor sent me to her."

Her pretty face melted with compassion. "A kidney stone! Oh, you poor dear! I hear those are awful. And you never told me."

I assumed a look of patient suffering. "It was nothing, just intense agony until the morphine kicked in. It happened while you weren't speaking to me." *Oh, no! Bad move, Jeff. Don't talk about that.*

"You mean while *you* weren't speaking to *me*, my darling."

That was technically true. I had avoided speaking to her because she broke up with me. After a little more than four weeks of that, we were kind of thrown together again by a murder.[1] It took Lynda another six months to figure out our relationship, but she finally did the sensible thing and proposed.[2] I didn't like to think much about our four weeks apart, even though I've written about it in two books, and right now I didn't want *her* to think about it. If she pressed me, I'd have to tell her the awful truth—that I'd spent that month pining away for her. My entire relationship with Trixie consisted of one office visit and a few casual meetings since then on the street or in a store. Admittedly, by my pathetic standards that practically qualified her as an ex-girlfriend. I wouldn't mind if Lynda thought that, as long as it didn't hurt

---

[1] See *No Police Like Holmes* (MX Publishing, 2011).
[2] See *Holmes Sweet Holmes* (MX Publishing, 2012).

her feelings or make her angry at me. A *tiny* bit of jealousy on her part might be a nice change.

That's what I was thinking as I found myself on the other end of the backstage area watching Triple M paint a bit of scenery for a later act. Sister Mary Margaret Malone wears her black hair chin length and parted in the middle, framing her cute face like parenthesis. It's a simple, yet becoming style that makes her look younger than her thirty-three years. Normally she wears plain dresses, a crucifix, and the symbol of her small community, the Daughters of St. Augustine. Tonight she was decked out in denim overalls.

"Pick up a paint brush or a hammer and help, Jeff," she said with her typical bright enthusiasm. "We can always use another hand."

"Not if it's Jeff's," Lynda said. "He'd wind up hurting himself—or somebody else." That was no put-down, just a fact. I'm all thumbs when it comes to that kind of stuff. The only manual labor I'm good at involves striking keyboards with my fingers.

Hovering behind Polly, towering over her five-six height, was a young man with a shaved head. He had a row of studs in each of his ears and snake tattoos on his bulging forearms. This must be Triple M's latest stray, the young man she'd met in her part-time job as jail chaplain and was trying to save. There was something of the loyal puppy dog about him. I remembered that later, after the murder.

I looked around at the unfinished scenery—canvas waiting to be painted and boards waiting to be nailed. "It's hard to believe this is all going to come together to make a play by the end of the week."

"It will, though," Triple M said.

And it did.

Mac came on stage as Mycroft early in the first act, wearing a vest and a frock coat along with one of his signature bow ties. I have to admit that he scowled magnificently, giving his freshly shaved chins a nice workout. "A most annoying business, Sherlock," he growled. I vaguely recognized the words as being from "The Adventure of the Bruce-Partington Plans," which I had read the night before. "I extremely dislike altering my habits, but the powers that be would take no denial. In the present state of Siam it is most awkward that I should be away from the office. But it is a real crisis. I have never seen the Prime Minister so upset. As to the Admiralty—it is buzzing like an overturned bee-hive."

I tweeted: *"Professor McCabe marvelous as Mycroft in 1895. Play runs all weekend and next."* I never pass up a chance to promote the college or someone associated with it.

In the play, as in the short story, Holmes informs Watson before his older brother's arrival that Mycroft is so important to the British government that "at times he *is* the British government." In the play, he is also the head of British secret service, which works in well with the original story line, and he's familiarly known to his subordinates by his first initial, M. (Yes, that song you hear in your head is the James Bond theme.)

The play closely follows the story in most respects, with some additions from other stories. When Holmes and Watson burgle a spy's apartment to get evidence, for instance, that's from the story. But some of the action and dialogue around the second-story work are borrowed from another Holmes yarn, "The Adventure of Charles Augustus Milverton."

On opening night, that was the last scene I got to see before leaving the theater.

Jonathan Hawes, in the person of Holmes, paused as if hearing something and cried out in a loud whisper, "Someone's coming! It may be the police. Quick, Watson—out the window!" And just at that moment everybody in the theater could hear a police siren. A mild chuckle passed through the audience as the crowd recognized the irony. The sound got louder and louder. *It must be close*, I thought. And then, just when it sounded like it was in the hall itself, it stopped dead.

Before I knew it, Lynda was out of her seat. For all my teasing, I'd always known she would never stop being a shoe leather journalist. It was in her DNA. There was a story, and she was on it. I followed her out of the darkened theater.

We quickly determined that the police chief's cruiser was pulled to the back of the theater. Although the siren had been turned off, the red light atop the vehicle was still rotating to create almost a strobe effect. Triple M's young friend, the dude with the ear piercings and tattoos, stood staring down at Oscar Hummel.

Erin's police chief was on his knees next to a crumpled body. A cell phone lay on the ground near the right hand. With a shock only partly due to the surreal circumstances, I recognized the apparently dead body in the angry glow of the flashing light. At the same time, I took in the awful spectacle of the blood oozing out of the corpse.

"This was no accident," I whispered to Lynda.

At least I thought I whispered.

"You're damned right it was no accident," Oscar said. "This man's been shot. Do any of you know him?"

"Yeah," I said. "I do."

Chapter Three
Wedding Plans

"How about the music?" I said. "Can we have Sinatra?"

"Sure," Lynda said. "I was also thinking Nora Jones and Nine Inch Nails."

"I like Paul Simon, too."

"Deal."

The negotiations were going well. That should have warned me. My life is never that smooth.

A week before the murder not a cloud on the horizon threatened my happiness. Lynda and I were discussing wedding plans as we huffed along on the elliptical machines at Nouveau Shape, the trendy gym right near campus, during our morning workout. Lynda had taken up running when she quit smoking during our relationship sabbatical. Later she added weekly taekwondo lessons, where she'd met Triple M. So it's not like she wasn't in good shape. Lynda is very shapely, in fact. But apparently she wanted to be in even better shape for the wedding and our honeymoon in Italy, so she'd started joining me at my morning workout. It turned out to be a great opportunity to work out the fine points of the upcoming nuptials.

At our ages, thirty-seven for me and thirty for Lynda, a lot of people have been through this at least once before. But we were newcomers at this, and Lynda had made it taekwondo clear that we had to get it right because neither of us was ever going to do it again.

Her curly hair was gathered into a ponytail and delightful rivulets of sweat stained her St. Benignus College workout T-shirt as she pumped her legs vigorously. She looked at me full-on. Oh, those eyes!

"Um, I need a favor, *tesoro mio.*"

Uh-oh. Incoming! Incoming! "My treasure" is a charming term of endearment in a beautiful language, and in Lynda's throaty voice it always seems packed with promise. But my radar was telling me that this time Lynda's Italian half was about to make me an offer I couldn't refuse.

"Of course. Anything your little heart desires, my precious kumquat. Just name it."

"Really? You're the best! Thanks, Jeff."

Damn. Why do I always have to be such a smartass?

"You're certainly welcome, oh love of my life. But do you mind if I ask—I mean, if it's not a secret or anything— what did I just agree to?"

She got off the elliptical machine and started to stretch. I think she was trying to distract me. It worked. When she finally figured out that she was going to have to tell me eventually, she pushed it all out there at once:

"You're going to move out of your apartment next week so that my father will have a place to stay when he comes in for the wedding and I know what that means to you and I really appreciate it."

She stopped stretching and kissed me on the lips, possibly to keep me from responding. I let her have her way with me for a while as I tried to process this announcement that was shocking on so many levels. First, I wasn't ready to move out of my carriage house apartment above Mac's garage. It had been my home ever since Mac and my sister Kate had bought the old house. Lynda had even agreed that we would live there together for a transitional period after the honeymoon while we looked for a place of our own to buy. Interest rates and home prices were both low, and I had substantial savings (Lynda not so much), so buying seemed the way to go—but not right away.

Even more shocking than the news that I just agreed to evict myself, was that I was making way for the Colonel, Lynda's father. My sweet fiancée and I had made good use of our engagement to share our hopes, dreams, fears, and secrets more than we had in all the years before. But Lynda's family was still a closed book to me. Her parents had met when her mother was in the Army. They had married young and divorced young. Lynda seemed to have been largely raised by Nonna, her late Italian grandmother, whom she loved very much. Her relationship with her father, Jake, was not close and her bond with her mother, Lucy, was troubled. That's about all I knew. *Just one big happy family! I can't wait to join it!*

On the pothole-laden rode to our own engagement, Lynda had told me many times that she didn't want to make the mistakes that her parents had made. But as to what those mistakes were, she'd never been specific. It seemed to be difficult for her to talk about. I was patiently waiting for the rest of the story. It was only a couple of months ago that she'd talked about her sister for the first time. In a conversation over lunch one day she'd casually referred to herself as the ugly duckling of the family.

"Wow, I'd like to see the other women," I'd said with a chuckle, thinking she was just being modest.

"I think I have a picture of Emma. She's my sister."

This was news to me. Lynda rooted around in her purse and pulled out a photo of a young woman with a big smile. Emma Teal also had hair the color of dark honey, but more wavy than curly like Lynda's. And she was gorgeous. That didn't make Lynda an ugly duckling, but I could see where my beloved was coming from with her self-description. Now I was in a pickle. How enthusiastic could I be about my future sister-in-law's physical charms without getting myself into trouble? Lynda didn't seem to mind my occasional off-handed comment about another woman's pulchritude, but maybe there was a sibling rivalry with her sister that I didn't know about. I settled on a middle course.

"She's certainly attractive," I conceded. "What does she do?" *Model? TV news anchor? Game show letter-turner?*

"Emma is a librarian at Midwestern State University in Chicago. She's six years younger than me and I don't know her all that well. But we're Facebook friends. I'm going to invite her to the wedding."

I had known that Lynda's parents would be coming to the wedding, or at least that they'd be invited, but the idea that they would be descending on me was a bolt out of the blue. "I'm glad your mom and dad are coming"—*maybe I'll finally find out what your deal is with them*—"but why does the Colonel have to stay at my place?"

Lynda picked up a twenty-pound weight and curled it, showing off her muscles. Was that a threat? "My father wants to stay near my mother. Apparently Emma told him that Lucy is staying in Mac's mother-in-law suite." *I wish she'd told me; I wish somebody had told me.*

"But your parents have been divorced since you were three years old."

She pumped harder. "Right. And Emma's twenty-four. Do the math."

Let's see. You're thirty, parents divorced twenty-seven years ago . . . Uh-oh. "You mean your father isn't Emma's father?"

"No, my dear, sweet, innocent nitwit. I mean that for all these years my parents have had what you might call an open divorce. They, shall we say, reconnect periodically. Thus, Emma."

"That's, uh, unusual."

"No, it's weird and it's wrong, but it's them. Their relationship is very passionate. When they get together they can barely keep their hands off of each other, much less their eyes. It's kind of icky to watch. Then within a few days, a week at the most, it all goes *ka-boom*. The passion explodes into major drama—shouting, throwing things, curses in Italian, the whole Richard Burton-Elizabeth Taylor bit. My father's jealousy always gets the best of him. He keeps a scrapbook of all my mother's lovers. And it's a big one."

"I could see where that could cause some tension." My head was spinning faster than a pinwheel on a windy day. I was also feeling unjustly accused in retrospect. Lynda used to say *I* was jealous. I was a piker compared to the Colonel. I'd never even thought of Lynda's old boyfriends. She must have had some, right? *I wonder who they were? I wonder how many*—

"So I'm sure he wants to stay close to her so he can keep an eye out," Lynda was saying, "but he's also hoping to seduce her." The way Lynda was gripping the weight, I was glad her hand wasn't around my neck. This was the most revealing information she'd ever shared about her parents, and it was taking a toll on her.

"Okay, the picture is starting to come into focus," I said. "But why is your mother staying at Mac's place to begin with? Couldn't she stay at the Winfield or the Harridan—those are very nice hotels."

"My father isn't the only one who wants to keep an eye on my mother, Jeff. I want to make sure that woman doesn't do something Richter-scale outrageous that threatens my wedding."

"You're getting married? What a coincidence—so am I!"

"Of course it's *our* wedding, darling, but I'm the one everybody will be looking at." *Damn, I can't argue with that.* "If your parents were coming, I'm sure that Mac and Kate would have insisted they stay in the suite. But since they aren't, I think the suite will be almost big enough for mother's wardrobe and makeup. Plus, Kate promised to watch her closely."

Kate and Lynda had grown much closer in a sisterly way over the past several months. Mac had always been fond of Lynda as well.

I'd been hoping since the engagement that my parents would be able to attend despite the arthritis that put my mother in a wheelchair almost eight years ago. But Dad had decided that the logistics of getting here from Virginia were just too much for him to handle.

"Well, I guess I'll just have to stay at your place," I said with a sigh of resignation.

Lynda set down her weight and kissed me on the lips, wrapping her arms around me. She was sweaty, but I didn't care.

"Nice try, big guy," she said when we'd finally disentangled, "but I need my beauty sleep so I'll look my best for the wedding. I was thinking maybe you could stay at Shamrocks & Ivy."

"Sounds like an Irish law firm."

"It's a bed and breakfast on College Street, very close to your office. You told me once you like B&Bs. I know there's room in this one because Polly has a friend staying there for a couple of days next week and he was told there's only one other guest."

"Wouldn't it be kind of expensive to stay at a B&B that long?"

"Cheapskate," my adoring fiancée responded. "This place is amazingly reasonable. I checked. Besides, you still have your First Communion money."

Apparently this was supposed to be a witticism suggesting that I could hold onto a dollar, which is both true and admirable. I thought the joke fell somewhat flat, however, considering that my First Communion had been less than a month before. But I let that pass. Once the Shamrocks & Ivy idea sunk in, it did have a certain appeal at the right price.

"I've never been to a B&B here in town," I said. "I'll pretend like I'm on vacation. It could be fun."

It wasn't.

Chapter Four
Mamma Mia!

One of the proofs that I am a reasonably normal human being, in spite of certain other evidence to the contrary, is that I hate going to the airport. But when Lynda asked me to accompany her to Greater Cincinnati/ Northern Kentucky International on Wednesday of the following week, the day before the premier of *1895*, I was happy to say yes. She was going to pick up her mother and she said she needed me for moral support. It's nice to be needed. It would also be nice to finally meet this mystery mamma, all of my subtle attempts to wheedle more info about her out of Lynda having failed.

So Lynda picked me up at work. On my way out of the office, I warned my administrative assistant, the irreplaceable Aneliese Pokorny—a.k.a. Popcorn—that I would be taking a long lunch. Of course, I would also be looking at my office e-mail on my iPhone during the drive in both directions, so it wasn't like I was really leaving work.

The Greater Cincinnati/Northern Kentucky International Airport is on the Kentucky side of the river. Erin has its own municipal airport, but that's just for small-fry planes. We took the ferry across the river and were there in less than an hour.

Waiting for somebody at the airport is probably the same from Northern Kentucky to North Korea. It's boring all the way until that exciting moment when you see the person you're waiting for. This time I wouldn't even know the person I was waiting for until Lynda pointed her out. I suspected that she would look something like Lynda, and I was quite sure that she would be very easy on the eyes for an older woman.

Her flight from New York was due at 1:05 P.M. and it was on time, according to the screen.

"So, she lives in New York?" I asked.

"For now. She moves around a lot. She always moved around a lot. So did my father, of course."

Wow, you're letting it all hang out. The mystery is being unpeeled like an onion.

Passengers came streaming out in bunches. You could never be sure if this was the plane you were waiting for or not because five planes may have just landed within a few minutes. So I kept watching, looking for tallish women with honey-blonde hair. Lynda and I were holding hands. My stomach was a bit tense and it grew more so when Lynda's squeeze tightened into a death grip.

A woman was waving to Lynda. She was decked out in what appeared to be the crown jewels of some small European country and a designer dress worth about the same as my 403(b) pension savings.

"That's your mother?"

"Yessss," Lynda hissed.

"Good heavens, do you realize she looks just like Lucia Schiaparelli?"

"That's because she *is*," Lynda said between clenched teeth. "And quit drooling, dammit."

Yes, *that* Lucia Schiaparelli, the most famous model of her era. "The Face That Launched a Thousand Dreams," *Vanity Fair* had called her in a profile on her recent fiftieth birthday. The rest of her body wasn't bad either. Everybody knew that because we'd seen most of it *sans* clothing in the iconic ad of her career, the commercial where she stood on a big shell in homage to Botticelli's *Birth of Venus*. It got millions of hits on YouTube and sold even more bottles of Birth of Venus perfume. And Lucia—her first name was often sufficient—was already at the half-century mark when the commercial was made. One magic evening, celebrating our engagement at Ricoletti's Ristorante, Lynda had reminded me of La Schiaparelli. It was beyond imagining then that I was seeing a family resemblance.

The model half-ran toward Lynda, which is about the best most women can do in four-inch spike heels with toes like sharpened pencils. Even with the heels she was barely Lynda's height in flats, much shorter than she looked on television.

"Lynda, *carina!*" she yelled. She put her arms around her daughter in a not-quite-hug, as if she had freshly painted fingernails that she was afraid of spoiling. Maybe she did, but I wasn't looking at her fingernails. Even close up, she was still a stop-you-in-your-tracks beauty, like her countrywoman Sophia Loren. Time leaves its mark on everyone, but the woman in front of me was a living advertisement for her new *Lucia!* line of makeup for mature women. And the sands of time hadn't redistributed her hourglass figure one bit; the deep neckline of her dress left no doubt about that.

"It's good to see you, Lucia," Lynda said, giving the name its Italian pronunciation. I'm almost sure her nose started growing.

"You look *meravigliosa*, darling—not a day over thirty-one," Lucia went on. I won't try to replicate the Italian flavoring in her pronunciation. "But I think you like your pasta a little much, eh? You have gained a few pounds, I think. Well, no matter. I have the perfect diet for you. You'll be in shape by the wedding. And your outfit! It's wonderful! How amazing what you can find at Goodwill. I think I have a few things you might like. We'll be the same size after the diet."

Sixty seconds after this woman first opened her mouth I was starting to understand why Lynda never wore that Birth of Venus perfume that I bought her at great expense. I was also feeling a little miffed on my own account. *I* was the one wearing a sport coat I bought for a dollar-fifty at the St. Vincent de Paul thrift store. (It was half-price day.) Why not let somebody else take the depreciation? Lynda, on the other hand, looked wonderful in a simple white crepe dress with a turned-up collar and a belt at the waste. Against her dark skin the effect was stunning. Her jewelry was restricted to her emerald engagement ring and a necklace with a colorful enamel butterfly. If she were wearing earrings they were covered by her curly blonde hair, which today was hanging free. Lynda's nose is a little crooked and her mouth a tad too big. I think she's the most beautiful woman in the world.

"And as for your crow's feet—"

"Mother," Lynda interrupted, "this is my fiancé, Jeff."

"Of course he is!" Lucia exclaimed. "You lucky girl! You never told me he was so handsome!" Well, she clearly had good taste in men. I suppose that was the problem. "You must give Lucia a kiss!"

I glanced sideways at Lynda. She rolled her eyes. That was not full-speed-ahead body language, but what could I do? Not wanting to be rude, I planted one on the icon's cheek and said, "It's so nice to meet you Signora Schiaparelli. I've heard so much about you." *And none of it came from Lynda.* That exotic scent she gave off must have been Birth of Venus; I'd never smelled it before. Was it really legal? Did people get arrested for driving under its influence?

Lucia gave me a hug that was the real thing, not the perfunctory version she'd doled out to Lynda, then stepped back while still holding on to my shoulders. "Don't believe everything you hear, my dear. Only half of it is true—the naughty half, of course. But you must call me Lucia. I will simply feel too old if you call me 'Mamma.'"

"We'd better get your luggage, Mamma," Lynda said with a kind of forced cheerfulness.

La Schiaparelli had four bags, each one roughly half the size of the island of Manhattan and a real pain to fit into Lynda's Mustang. That seemed like a lot until I realized that she probably wasn't planning to wear the same outfit twice during her stay. She might wear more than one on some days. It must be tough being a supermodel.

"Why don't you sit in the back seat with me, Jeff?" my future mother-in-law suggested. *My, what big eyes you have, Grandma!* They were deep brown, but without Lynda's unique gold flecks. Was she really a grandma? The thought seemed unthinkable, but Emma could have three kids for all I knew. Never mind that, though, the lady had asked me a question. (Why did my train of thought keep running off the tracks around this woman?) "We can get acquainted," she added.

The idea did have its appeal. I wouldn't run away from La Loren, either.

"You can get acquainted perfectly well with Jeff sitting up front," Lynda told her mother before I could respond. *That's just what I was going to say, my beloved.*

Lucia sighed theatrically. "You spoil all my fun, Lynda, as usual. Children are such a trial sometimes." The pouty look on her face was kind of cute.

In the car, I watched her in the rear view mirror. Even with one of her bags parked in the other seat back there she managed to look like she was occupying the chaise lounge in some count's eighteenth-century manor.

"So, tell me all about yourself, Jeff. Where do you spend your days being handsome?"

I could get used to this. The trip back to Mac's would have been very pleasant if Lynda hadn't been so jerky at the wheel.

It was almost 2:30 when we reached the house on Half Moon Street. Mac was home from slaving away at the college and not yet departed for dress rehearsal at the Lyceum. Kate, being a stay-at-home mom to three children as well as an artist, was also in residence. My big sister is almost six feet tall with hair as red as mine, but much longer and generally piled on top. They came to greet us at the door.

"What a cute little house!" Lucia exclaimed. The McCabe residence has ten or twelve rooms. "You were very kind to invite me."

"It's our pleasure to host Lynda's mother," Kate assured her. "She is truly like a sister to me. I'm Kate."

"And I am Sebastian McCabe," my brother-in-law announced, although he didn't look like himself with his clean-shaven face. "*È un gran piacere di conoscervi, signora.*" He bent over, the show-off. I thought he was going to take her hand and kiss it, and I bet she did too. Instead, he produced a rose in his hand out of nowhere and presented it to my future mother-in-law with a flourish.

Lucia gave a little squeal of delight. "You are a magician. How enchanting! You remind me of dear Orson, except that he had a beard. I met him only once. I was very young and he was very old but he still made a pass at me, the naughty boy." *I bet it was a completed pass.*

"Would you like to freshen up from your trip?" Kate asked Lucia.

"*Davvero*, that is exactly what I would like right now."

"Jeff and I will bring in your bags," Lynda said. "Then we have to get back to our jobs."

"Yes, yes, you do that." She made a shooing motion with her hands. "Don't worry about Lucia. I'll be fine." *It's not Lucia that we're worried about.* "We'll spend some time together later. I'm sure we'll have a wonderful visit."

Lynda didn't look so sure.

Chapter Five
Daddy Dearest

"Well," Lynda said, driving me back to my office, "now you know."

"I know more than I did before, but not as much as I'd like. Was this whole mystery thing just because you didn't want to tell me that your mother is somebody famous?"

"She's not just famous," Lynda said. "She's also infamous. You remember my father's scrapbook that I told you about, the one about her lovers? It must be in multiple volumes by now."

I shook my head. "I'm no expert on La Schiaparelli's love life. The only time I read *People* magazine is standing in line at the grocery store checkout counter. I didn't even read the *Vanity Fair* piece. But I can understand why your feelings for her aren't the warmest. Now maybe you can explain why you didn't just give me the scoop on her a long time ago. I'm supposed to be your unlimited partner, remember?"

That was pretty heavy, I know, but we were dealing with heavy stuff like trust, openness, and signing up for the long haul.

Lynda bit her lip and stared straight ahead at the road. "I knew that if we stayed together you'd meet her some day. I wanted you to see for yourself what she's like and form your own impression. I didn't want to poison your mind in advance. And look what happened—she practically seduced my fiancé."

"You can relax about that, sweetheart. My feelings for your mother are purely physical."

"That does *not* help." Why is it that her throaty voice is at its sexiest just when amorous thoughts are the farthest thing from her mind? A tear rolled down her face. She sniffed.

"Hey, Lyn, I was just trying to lighten the mood. What's the matter?" In my professional capacity, I never say the wrong thing. After working hours, my record is more mixed.

"From the time I was eighteen years old until I went to college and never lived with her again she stole every boyfriend I brought home," Lynda said. "She was a cougar before cougar was cool."

Wow. What do I say to that? It took me a few seconds to come up with:

"That must have been hard, competing with your mother."

"There was no competition. She was glamorous, already a little bit famous, and she was willing to give the boys something I wouldn't." *Coo-coo-ka-choo, Mrs. Robinson!*

"Well, you're not going to lose this boyfriend." I took her hand, ignoring the fact that this is a dangerous thing to do when somebody is driving. "You're stuck with me, kid."

She didn't say anything, didn't need to. She brought my left hand up to her lips and kissed it.

I moved the conversation into less emotionally charged territory. "I thought your parents were both in the Army."

"They were." The short drive to my office was over. Lynda pulled into the lot and parked the Mustang. "Lucia came to the U.S. with my grandparents when she was ten. She was such a wild kid that Nonna lit candles in thanksgiving when Lucia turned eighteen and joined the Army. When I came along Nonna took that as proof that her hellion was settling down. That worked for a couple of years until she won some kind of military pin-up contest—I think it was Miss Camouflage, of which she wasn't wearing any—and started modeling.

"I'm not really sure why she took me with her when she left my father. I've already told you how Nonna really did all the heavy lifting in rearing me. Lucia did a lot of traveling for her career. She never minded when Nonna took me off to Italy for months at a time during the summer. Sometimes I think my dad would have tried to get custody of me, and later Emma, if he hadn't been posted all over the globe."

She shook her head. "The poor man never got over my mother, you know. I almost didn't either. It took me a long time to convince myself that history isn't destiny and we can do better than they did."

"I'm sure we can," I said stoutly.

"Just don't make one false move. Remember, I know martial arts." *Such a kidder. You are kidding, aren't you, Lyn?*

"What about your father? He isn't, for example, Arnold Schwarzenegger, is he? No, don't tell me. That might as well be a surprise, too."

Lynda's father was not Arnold Schwarzenegger. I met him late that afternoon after he'd driven in from Washington.

But first I dropped by my office. I'm always wary of spending too much time away, despite being in constant contact by iPhone. I'm afraid that Popcorn will figure out that she can run the place without me better than I ever could without her. Oscar Hummel, not normally known for his apt turn of phrase, once appropriately referred to my administrative assistant as "a neat little package." She's just under five feet tall, dyed blonde, almost fifty and ignoring it. I realized with a start that she was Lucia's generation, and must have viewed her as either a rival or as a role model much of her adult life.

"So what's the mother-in-law-to-be like?" she asked.

"Unbelievable."

I could have left it at that. But knowing the widow Pokorny's addiction to celebrity magazines and the more-than-suggestive romance novels of Rosamund DeLacey, I thought it would be cruel not to expound.

"Lynda's mother is Lucia Schiaparelli. I have orders not to call her 'Mamma,' not that I would."

It took me almost ten minutes to convince Popcorn that I wasn't joking and the rest of the afternoon to describe Lucia's clothes, jewelry, smells, accent, and the way she hugged me. As a special favor, I pulled out my poetic license and used it to pump a little drama into the part where she invited me to sit in the back seat with her. Popcorn was on the edge of her seat as I described her highly seductive voice and so forth.

"Get out of town!" she gasped. "How did Lynda react?"

"She grabbed me out of the vamp's clutches and pulled me into the front seat."

"Somehow I doubt that."

"Let's not quibble over semantics. Lynda made it clear she wanted me in the front seat and that's where I sat. I know what's good for me."

At quitting time I pedaled my Schwinn back to the carriage house with a certain melancholy, knowing that my bags were packed. Tonight I would be turning over my home temporarily to a future father-in-law who remained a mystery to me.

As I approached I saw Lynda standing in the driveway talking to a man almost my height with a ramrod straight posture that made him seem taller. Although casually dressed in a light windbreaker, he seemed more GQ than GI. When I got closer I saw that he was impossibly handsome, like George Clooney with grayer hair, iron gray. No wonder the Teal girls were so beauteous—they had inherited attractive genes from both sides of the family tree.

Lynda's arms were folded under her ample bosom, which students of body language could interpret as sending messages of resistance. But I think she was just resting her arms as she leaned against a midnight blue Buick Lucerne that I assumed belonged to the Colonel. (The 2012 Buick looked embarrassed, by the way, sitting next to my fourteen-year-old lime green Beetle.) The Colonel was a few feet away, not into her space in the manner of people who are really close, but

Lynda looked happy. She had a smile on her face and a sparkle in her eye. It took me a moment to realize that the emotion I was feeling was jealousy.

That disappeared like fog in the sunshine when I saw her smile widen at the sight of me.

"Hi, Jeff! Meet Daddy."

I parked the bike and didn't wait for Lynda to pronounce names. "Good to meet you, sir," I said, offering my hand. I thought that sounded suitably military.

"Hi, Jeff," he said. His handshake was firm, manly. I liked the fact that he didn't crush my hand to show me how macho he was. "Any future husband of my daughter is a future son-in-law of mine." *Well, I can't argue with that, sir.* Small talk didn't seem to be his big suit, but I didn't hold that against him. "Thanks for the loan of the apartment. I really appreciate it."

Don't thank me; it wasn't my idea. "It's no trouble at all, Colonel." *Your daughter for my apartment isn't a bad trade.* But even though he would be giving away his daughter at the wedding, it didn't seem like Jake Teal had ever really had her to give away. And yet they seemed to get along. "Let me show you around the place."

I took him, and Lynda, up the seventeen steps to my apartment above the garage. It only took about five minutes to show him the living room, the bedroom, the spare room, the bathroom, and the tiny kitchen.

"It's not much," I said. "I hope you're not cramped."

"Oh, I'll be fine," he assured me. "Before I went to the Pentagon I lived in a tent in Afghanistan for two years, and that wasn't my worst crib."

It was hard to read the expression on Lynda's face for sure, but I'm guessing it was pride.

My packed suitcases and a few other bags standing the living room caught the Colonel's eye as we ended the tour where we'd begun. "Let me give you a hand with all that."

There was a trace of the south in his speech, an accent worn smooth by years of rubbing up against Yankees. I'd been through that myself. What Lynda used to call my "cute Virginia drawl" is mostly gone, she says, except when I'm nervous.

I had the feeling the Colonel could pick up two suitcases in one hand and me in the other, but he was no show-off. He picked up one bag in each hand. As he did so his windbreaker rode up and I caught site of something in his belt.

"Is that a gun?" I asked, pointing.

He looked, as if unsure. "No, son, that's a firearm."

"Ah, good." *Two can play at this game.* "I'm glad to hear that, sir, because we have a concealed carry law in Ohio that says you need a license to carry a concealed weapon. So if you don't have a license that would be a problem."

The Colonel pulled back his windbreaker to give me a better look at the firearm. "You saw that, right?"

"Yes, sir."

"Then it wasn't concealed."

I looked at Lynda, who shrugged. Max Cutter would love this guy. I wasn't sure what to think.

Chapter Six
Shamrocks & Ivy

A few hours later Mac was heading to dress rehearsal, Kate was making sure the three kids had their homework done, Lynda was with her parents, and I was taking my bags into my temporary new quarters at the Shamrocks & Ivy Bed and Breakfast.

The adults—if you count Mac as an adult—had all dined out together at Lucia's insistence. Ricoletti's Ristorante is both authentically Italian and the most elegant eatery in Erin.

Usually size and personality make Sebastian McCabe the dominant figure at any gathering around a table, as I have written elsewhere, but not this time. All eyes were on La Schiaparelli, especially those of her ex-husband. The way he looked at her, you would have thought they were on their honeymoon. It was the look of love, certainly, and maybe something akin to adoration. She deigned to look at him only occasionally, but something told me she was just being coy— that the attraction wasn't one-sided.

When Enzo Ricoletti himself got word that Lucia was in the house, shortly after we ordered our meals, he suddenly appeared at our table like the Roadrunner popping up in a Warner Bros. cartoon. He didn't beep-beep, but he did spew out a flow of Italian *("Incantevole!" "Bellessima!")* that had Lynda rolling her eyes and downing her Knob Creek Manhattan. Clearly, my bride-to-be remained impervious to her mother's charms. As for Mac and Kate, I wasn't sure how they were reading their new houseguest.

Lucia talked all through dinner so much about her latest project, a new line of retro clothing from Macy's, and her recent vacation on the Italian Riviera ("I ran into Leonardo—such a charming boy, I wish he would choose better scripts") that I started to feel sorry for the Colonel. Never mind that he was hanging on every word. I decided to give him his time in the spotlight. "So," I said when Lucia paused long enough to sip a glass of sixty-dollar-a-bottle wine from an eight-hundred-year-old Tuscan winery, "what's new at the Pentagon, Colonel?"

"The usual challenges of waging war and forging peace, I'm sure. But that's not my concern anymore. I've retired."

That was news to me. I would have asked what he was going to do now if Enzo hadn't showed up to force his homemade cannoli on us. I can never eat cannoli without thinking of that great line from *The Godfather*, "Leave the gun. Take the cannoli." But that doesn't mean I can never eat it. Sure, it's not especially healthful, but the delicious salmon I'd just eaten was. I picked out the candied cherries on the end to reduce the calories. Lynda ate them, shooting me a look that dared me to comment. I didn't.

After cannoli and cappuccino (decaf for me), the party broke up. Lynda walked me to my car.

"Does your father always carry a gun?" I asked.

"He prefers to think of it as a firearm. That's his Beretta." *Beretta? Wasn't that James Bond's first gun, before M took it away and gave him the PPK?* "He's had it for years."

"Well, I hope he doesn't get mad at something and shoot up my apartment." *Or your mother.*

"Don't be silly."

Why had this habit of her father never come up when Lynda complained about the, quote, macho bullshit, in the Max Cutter private eye novels I wrote year after year without achieving publication? Maybe her father was *why* she complained. *Sigmund Freud, call your office.*

I gave Lynda a lingering kiss, then got into my car and drove gloomily to the B&B where I would be living for the remainder of my bachelorhood.

Shamrocks & Ivy was a Victorian Painted Lady. According to the website, it had been a stop on the Underground Railroad, like the McCabe house and so many others in this Ohio River town. As the son of a successful Realtor, I've always been interested in houses. This was a nice one. Close up, though, I could see that the multi-colored paint job that gave the style of house its name was a couple of years overdue for a sprucing up. *No wonder the cost was so cheap. I hope the breakfast is good.*

When I pulled up in my car, I immediately faced a parking dilemma. I usually pedal my Schwinn to work, and I was still close enough to do that. So by parking in the driveway I would block in one of the two cars in front of the slightly leaning detached garage. I decided not to worry because I could move my car in the morning. So I pulled behind a Ford Fusion with a kid's car seat in the back. The other car was a BMW, not new but in excellent condition.

I rang the doorbell. After waiting about a minute, I was about to ring it again when a man in suspenders opened the door. He was Social Security age, with soft white hair and a goatee. I was just about to make him hate me at first sight by saying I didn't want any of his fried chicken, but I caught myself in time.

"Good evening. Mr. Apple? I'm Jeff Cody." That was better.

"Of course, of course." He opened the door wide. "Welcome to Erin. How was your trip?"

"Actually, I live here. My trip was about five minutes from Ricoletti's."

I'd already explained the whole rigmarole to his wife when I'd made the reservation, but I treated him to the story as well. For me it wasn't improved any by having met the Colonel and Lucia.

George Apple showed me the parlor, the dining room where I'd be eating breakfast every day, and the kitchen. He explained apologetically that his wife was working on a play tonight at that new theater. I allowed as how I knew something about that.

"Well, you get settled in," he said. "If there's anything you need, just ask. I'll be in the parlor, waiting up for Sally."

There was one bedroom downstairs, where the Apples lived, and three upstairs. George showed me to mine. It was spacious enough, no complaint there. And it would be silly to carp that everything was old and a bit shopworn, even the television set. "Vintage" was the way the website had described it, fairly enough. The floors were uneven. The wallpapered walls were decorated with Victorian-era photos and prints. The drapes had a shamrock design. Women's lingerie, hats, and dresses hung from hooks and hangers around the room. *If I were a cross-dresser, I'd be in paradise.* The bathroom, also big, had a clawfoot tub and a big showerhead, added later, that reminded me of a sunflower.

I plopped down on the bed, which had a canopy, and leaned against a fluffy pillow. A dresser with a mirror lay to my right, with an antique water jug sitting on it. In front of me was a bricked-up fireplace, with a desk and a small TV to the left of that. Seeing the desk made me realize that I'd forgotten to bring my laptop.

I'd always liked bed and breakfasts. This one was a little quaint for my tastes, but that wasn't the real problem. I was lonely. Sure, I've lived alone for years—but just a few yards away from my sister and brother-in-law. That's not *really* alone. Now I was, both alone and lonely, and especially lonely for Lynda. But I knew that if I called her I'd be even lonelier. So I sent her a text:

JEFF: *I miss you.*

LYNDA: U *just left me like 34 minutes ago*

JEFF: *Seems longer. Time flies when you're having fun, but I'm not. And I miss my lapdance.*
LYNDA: *Lapdance?? Who do u hav me confused with???*
JEFF: *I meant laptop. Stupid autocorrect!!! Did I mention I miss you?*
LYNDA: *Buck up. Be a man*
JEFF: *Give me the chance!*
LYNDA: *I happen to think i'm worth waiting for*

Well, she had me there. The conversation got very personal for a while before drifting into a recap of the evening (my suggestion that her mother wasn't so bad met with stony silence), then ended with my description of the B&B room. I should have just called her and saved some time. By the time we posted affectionate signoffs, I was still lonely but felt more cheerful about it.

Thinking honeymoon thoughts, I used the iPhone to check the weather in Rome, Florence, and Venice, the cities that awaited us at the end of the month. *Looking good!* That took a while, but was a lot of fun.

Finished with that and uncomfortable with the silence in the unfamiliar surroundings, I turned on the television. One of the 24-hour cable stations was on. That was fine by me. I'm a bit of a news junkie, although sometimes I wonder why. It's all the same stuff, slightly shuffled. Tonight, for example, within ten minutes or so I got caught up on the baseball scores, the flap du jour in the seemingly endless presidential campaign season, the disappearance of a nine-month-old boy in Athens, Ohio, and street demonstrations in an Arab country I'd never heard of.

Ten minutes of that was enough to have me craving silence again, so I turned off the TV and hauled out my one-volume Doubleday edition of *The Complete Sherlock Holmes.* Mac had given it to me for a Christmas present years before, when we'd both been students at St. Benignus rather than its employees. Kate had suggested that I re-read "The Adventure of the Bruce-Partington Plans" to prepare for the play.

I got through it only with difficulty. That wasn't the story's fault. Even though I'm not an idolater of Sherlock Holmes, I'd give the tale high marks as a combination of detection, intrigue, and action. But my mind kept going back to the news report of the missing boy upstate in Athens. His name was Bart Cain. They'd issued an Amber Alert and were showing his cute picture on television.

He had disappeared the day before from his family home while he was supposed to be taking a nap. His parents were both professors at Ohio University, where Lynda had received her degree in journalism. His paternal grandfather was Ben Cain, master distiller of Louisville-based Old Ben Bourbon. He wasn't the original Benjamin F. Cain for whom the bourbon was named, but a direct descendent. My bourbon-loving fiancée could probably draw the whole family tree, or at least the main branches.

I'd followed enough stories like this to know that the poor kid was probably dead. In the unlikely event that he wasn't, he must be terrified, confused, and crying for his mommy and daddy. And his parents would be going through hell. This kind of thing happened all the time in cities and towns across America. This case was nationally newsworthy because of the prominence of the family, but it could have been any family. Alone in a strange room, that scared the hell out of me. Lynda and I hoped to give the McCabe children cousins in short order. Was I really ready for the perils of parenthood?

I didn't sleep so well that night.

Chapter Seven
Breakfast Club

In the morning I met the other guests and our hostess around the breakfast table.

Sally Apple reminded me of the Pillsbury doughboy, round and cheerful and wearing an apron, as she bustled about the kitchen making French toast casserole. Her dirty white hair looked like a well-used mop. I pegged her age in the sixties, roughly the same as her husband.

One guest sat at the long dining room table chatting with George Apple as I entered. He was in his mid-thirties, handsome, with closely cropped dark hair and a mustache. ". . . in the Army," he was telling George as I entered.

"Good morning," I wished both of them.

"Hi, I'm Bill Kirtland," said the guest.

"Oh, sure. Polly's friend." I caught myself just before referring to her as "Triple M," my private pet name for Sister Mary Margaret Malone. "Jeff Cody." I put out my hand and we did the "nice-to-meet-you" shake. Judging by the placemats on the table, one more guest would be joining us this morning. Each of our plates held a fruit cup starring half a grapefruit with a maraschino cherry artistically placed in the center.

"Coffee?" George asked with an eagerness that made me wonder whether he was expecting a tip.

"Decaf please."

He poured, then offered me milk out of a half-gallon plastic jug. I noted approvingly that it was skim milk.

"So you knew Polly from the Army, right?" I said to my fellow guest, making conversation. Lynda was, in theory, an army brat, although she hadn't lived with her father very long. I'd often thought that perhaps that was part of her connection to the good sister.

"Yeah. We dated for about three years."

Why did that surprise me? I knew the woman wasn't born a sister—she'd even been in the Army! Yet somehow I'd been thinking that this guy was a friend friend, not an ex-boyfriend friend. Kirtland seemed to read the expression on my face.

"We broke up a long time ago," he said. He forced a smile, showing a good set of teeth below his mustache. "Don't worry, she wasn't a nun then." He sipped coffee.

Actually, Triple M wasn't a nun; she was a religious sister. But only a show-off (such as Mac, for instance) would split that particular hair to a guy who probably wasn't interested. Groping around for a more acceptable response, I opted for the neutral, "Well, I'm sure she was glad to see you again. What brings you to Erin?"

"A little business trip," he said. "When I realized I'd be swinging by here I decided to stay a couple of nights and visit Polly. We've kept in touch on Facebook. I haven't seen her yet, though. That's today's project, along with a little antiquing and just taking in the town. I like small towns."

"What do you do?" I asked.

Kirtland paused from his grapefruit. "I'm kind of a security consultant, I guess you could say."

Mrs. Apple came through the dining room door, bearing the French toast casserole. Her husband, who had ducked out of the room, returned with what he assured us was warm maple syrup with pecans.

"Are you going to the play tonight?" Mrs. Apple asked Kirtland.

I'd noticed a copy of Kate's poster in the hallway when I'd come in last night.

"I heard about it," Kirtland said. "Polly told me she's working on the stage crew. But I hadn't really thought of going."

"Got anything better to do?" George asked.

"No, I guess I haven't at that. I'll ask Polly to get me a ticket."

"I can help with that," Mrs. Apple said. "I have a small part in the play, just a few lines near the beginning." *Aw, shucks.* "I'm Mrs. Hudson."

"Typecasting," I murmured.

"Good morning." It sounded like an order.

Our third guest had finally made her appearance. She was Asian, probably in her mid-forties, with a ramrod straight posture that made her look taller than her five-six or so. Her dark hair was long but pulled back tightly and held in place off her neck with a hair comb. She would have looked perfectly natural in a black and red satin dress with a mandarin collar and a slit up the side. Instead, she wore a business-like cream blouse, navy blue skirt, and matching jacket. I was sure she had a briefcase nearby.

"Good morning, Ms. Quong," Mrs. Apple said. "Your tea is ready."

"Thank you."

She seated herself without wrinkling her skirt.

"Ms. Quong is a long-termer," George said. "Been here a week. She just started at Gamble." Gamble Bank & Trust Co. is a homegrown financial institution that also has a few branches in adjoining counties.

I figured if somebody didn't say something fast, George would spill everything he knew about everybody there and that could get embarrassing. Maybe it already was for Ms. Quong. She was doing nothing to encourage his chattiness, such as volunteering information about herself. So I nominated myself to change the subject just as Mrs. Apple set a pot of tea in front of the banker.

"We were just talking about that play at the Lyceum, *1895*," I said. "Tonight's the opening. There are probably worse ways to waste your time, especially if you like Sherlock Holmes or mysteries."

She sipped her tea. "I'm sure it will be quite entertaining, and I do enjoy the theater. Unfortunately, I have a dinner engagement this evening." She spoke English so perfectly that I was almost certain it wasn't her native language, but she'd probably been speaking it so long she'd forgotten Chinese or whatever language she'd learned first.

"How do I get to St. Benignus?" Kirtland asked. Triple M works there as a campus minister. Her gig as a chaplain at the jail is a volunteer position.

"All roads lead to St. Benignus," I assured him with acceptable hyperbole.

George gave him a map anyway.

"Oh, and I noticed you've blocked me in, Jeff," Kirtland. "Will you be leaving soon?"

I would, but not in the VW. I told him I'd move it.

After that the conversation drifted off into the weather (predicted to be partly sunny today with a high near 70 degrees), the Cincinnati Reds, and the state of the economy (improving, but slowly).

Ms. Quong—somewhere along the line it had emerged that her first name was Amy—got up from the table first. She'd said little, but very politely. Since I also had a job to go to, I was next.

"Breakfast was fantastic," I told Mrs. Apple. *It was calorie-heavy, fat-laden, and should cause me to spend an extra hour at the gym to make up for it. I've really got to work on my self-control if I'm going to stay here until the wedding.*

As it turned out, I didn't even get to the gym for several days.

My parting words were to Bill Kirtland:

"It was good to meet you. Have a great day."

He didn't.

Chapter Eight
Scene of the Crime

"His name is Bill Kirtland," I said, looking down at the body on the concrete sidewalk behind the theater. "He's staying at a B&B called Shamrocks & Ivy."

"Polly's friend!" Lynda gasped.

I'd forgotten that she'd never met him.

I put my arm around her and pulled her close to me. We'd seen murdered bodies before—in fact, it was getting to be a damned annoying habit—but you never get used to it. The bullet had entered the back of his head. Truthfully, I didn't look too close. I knew it was Kirtland from the clothes he'd been wearing in the theater, jeans and V-neck sweater over a golf shirt.

"What's he doing in Erin?" Oscar demanded, as if I should know. And, of course, I did.

"He was passing this way on business and decided to stop and see Polly Malone. That's what he said at breakfast this morning."

Oscar gave me a "what the hell?" look.

"I'm staying at Shamrocks & Ivy, too."

"What happened—Mac kick you out?"

"Never mind, Oscar," I said. "You wouldn't believe it anyway."

"I already can't believe this, another murder in this town. I should have retired to someplace quiet—like maybe New York."

Oscar had been a desk sergeant in Dayton before coming to quiet Erin as police chief. Murder, mayhem, and Sebastian McCabe have dogged him almost ever since.

"Now they're shooting people in the streets," Oscar added. We were behind the theater, between the back of the building and the parking lot. This was Broadway Street, in the heart of downtown Erin, maybe five blocks away from any residence. "And where is my assistant chief? He's acting in a frickin' play!"

L. Jack Gibbons had been Oscar's right-hand man ever since the new chief arrived two years ago. Swallowing his disappointment at being passed over for chief himself, he'd proved an invaluable source of local lore to his boss as well as a solid officer, methodical and thorough. Oscar had recently done the right thing and given him the rank of lieutenant and the title of assistant chief, although for me it was hard not think of him still as Officer Gibbons.

For a minute I thought Oscar was going to take off his Cincinnati Reds cap and slap something with it in frustration. But he would never do that because it would expose his bald head.

"I suppose I might as well just call in McCabe and be done with it!"

(This was all one long rant that went very fast; I'm breaking it up to make it easy on you.)

One of Oscar's favorite pastimes his first year or so in town was reading Mac's Damon Devlin amateur detective novels and underlining all the parts that he thought were unrealistic. Then he'd argue with Mac, line by line. He was right, of course. Those stories are pure moonshine and fairy dust. My Max Cutter private eye novels are much more like real life. That's one difference between Mac's mysteries and mine. The other is that his get published and are sold in obscene quantities, while mine have yet to see print.

Lately I've been rethinking the whole enterprise of mystery writing. Getting up-close and personal with real murder victims—and real murderers—has taken some of the fun out of fiction for me. Maybe I should stick to true crime writing; I seemed to be getting plenty of material for that without even trying.

Mac himself professed to be chastened and changed by our last such adventure, but he did solve two murders. That proved that his first success in uncovering a killer was no fluke. Ever since the second case last fall, Oscar had evinced a reluctant deference to his former verbal sparring partner.

"Mac's in the play, too," I told Oscar. "He also wrote it." Details like that are likely to get by Oscar during baseball season. He didn't take the news well. I could almost see him struggling to keep from popping a blood vessel, and rightly so. A guy who can't see his shoes over his belt buckle shouldn't run that risk. "Lynda and I were in the audience ourselves until we heard the siren."

"When's this play over?"

"Based on the dress rehearsal," Lynda said, "I'd guess it only has another twenty minutes or so to go."

Oscar patted his breast pocket but found no pack of cigarettes there. He never does because he prefers to borrow them from friends instead of buying his own. Even after she quit smoking Lynda used to carry a pack in her purse for Oscar, a sop to his hatred of journalists, but she stopped that when she got promoted.

The chief looked over at Triple M's shadow, the young man with the shaved head and ear studs. He'd been standing to one side, nervously smoking a cigarette. Every time he brought up his hand to take a drag, the snake tattoos on his arm appeared to slither.

"You!" Oscar snapped.

His eyes opened like the electronic shutter on an iPhone camera. "Yessir!"

"You're Justin Bird, aren't you?"

The young man nodded guiltily.

"Lend me a smoke, will you?"

"Uh, sure."

Just as he handed it over, another flashing light split the night. A police car with a man and woman inside pulled up. Out jumped the male officer with a Nikon. I knew that crime scene photos would be next, but probably no fingerprint dusting in this particular situation.

"Thanks, kid," Oscar said. "Don't go anywhere. Talk to you in a minute."

"Yessir!"

Oscar went over to the cruiser and talked to his cops, pointing at various buildings. I held Lynda's hand. It was icy, even though the evening was seasonably mild. After a minute or two, the chief walked back to us.

"I think it was just one shot," he said. "Did you hear it?"

"No," Lynda said, "we only ran out of the play because we heard the sirens."

"Nobody else seems to have heard anything either, not that we know of," Oscar said.

"Then how did you know what happened?" I asked.

"We got a 911 call from him." He turned around. "Now where the hell did he go?"

"Who?" I asked.

"Justin Bird."

The young man was gone, and none of us had noticed when he'd slipped away.

"Hell's bells!" Oscar swore. "That kid was in my lockup a couple of months ago on a gun charge. Maybe I won't need Mac *or* Gibbons to close this case."

Chapter Nine
McCabe's Questions

Sebastian McCabe, still in costume as he stood near the covered body of Bill Kirtland, lit a cigar. His favorite vice, denied to him at home and in any public building, had not yet been outlawed outside. So, free to pollute his lungs and fill the night air with second-hand smoke, he went at it as he tried to imagine the murder.

For the first time in a murder case, he seemed subdued and reflective—not like a kid in a candy store. He'd evinced reluctance, possibly even genuine, to share his thoughts until Oscar insisted.

"It seems simple enough," he allowed. "Kirtland was standing here"—he stood there—"when the murderer approached from behind and shot him in the back of the head. His body folded like an accordion."

"Sure, sure," Oscar agreed. "Only way it could have happened. That's obvious."

"Yes." Mac imitated a chimney. "However, Sherlock Holmes once said there is nothing more misleading than an obvious fact. And there are some puzzling circumstances here. For example, that shot from behind does seem a bit odd, does it not?"

"How so?" He had Oscar hooked.

"Well, on the one hand, it does not indicate the shooting was spontaneous, the result of an argument. Victim and killer would have been facing each other in that case. On the other hand, it hardly seems that one could plan a murder assuming the victim would be accommodating enough to be standing in just the appropriate spot for a clean shot. Moreover, what was Kirtland doing out here while the play was still going on in there? Surely my performance was not that discreditable."

"Maybe it was a crime of opportunity," Oscar said. "The kid, Justin Bird, said he snuck out to grab a smoke and found the body. Maybe he *did* go out to grab a smoke and saw Kirtland, only he was still alive until Justin made him otherwise."

"You're sure he did it?" Lynda said.

"He ran. We're calling him a person of interest." I don't know whether Oscar picked that up from CNN or *CSI*. He watches both.

"Motive?" Mac asked.

Oscar shrugged. "Who knows? Maybe robbery, maybe something that wouldn't make sense to anybody else. The kid's kind of strange and he likes to shoot guns when he's mad. I had him as a guest a while back over a little matter of emptying a pistol at a school bus."

"So after firing the fatal shot, he called 911 to report the crime so that you would know he was on the scene?" Mac said. "And did I understand you correctly, Oscar, that no one else heard the shot? This is a fairly busy section of downtown."

"Maybe Justin used some kind of sound suppressor, what you mystery writers call a silencer."

Mac raised a quizzical eyebrow. "He happened to bring not only a gun but a silencer to the theater tonight when he reported for work backstage?"

Oscar patted his shirt pocket futilely. "Maybe he shot through something else to muffle the sound. Sometimes wise guys use a liter bottle wrapped with duct tape around the mouth. Maybe he did that, or shot through something else. I don't know. You're being too logical."

Mac smiled faintly. "That is a flaw of which I have seldom been accused. At the moment, however, I admit the accusation. Logically, it seems to me that if Justin came out to smoke a cigarette, or for whatever reason, he would come out the back door or the side door. Neither exit would have afforded him a stealthy approach to Kirtland from the rear. What do you think, Lieutenant Gibbons?"

I'd almost forgotten that he was there. Medium in height, average in looks, middle-aged, Gibbons tends to blend into the background until you need him. He looked at the chief as if to silently ask whether it was okay to answer the question. Oscar gave an almost imperceptible nod.

"I see what you're saying, Professor McCabe, but I'm not sure you're right about the side door," Gibbons said. "From where the body fell, it looks like Mr. Kirtland wasn't standing right on the corner of the sidewalk and alley. I think whoever shot him could have been hiding behind the dumpster in the parking lot behind him to his right as he faced Market Street, or come out the side door of the theater and walked down the alley to come up behind him from his left, or crossed the alley between here and the funeral home."

Mac looked in the direction Kirtland was facing when he was shot—toward Market Street, which intersects Broadway. "I wonder why he was turned in that direction. What was he looking at?"

The only thing I could see was the back of the buildings on Market Street, including Jim Bridges' law offices, Bobbie McGee's Sports Bar, Happy Homes Realty, and the Hawes & Holder Funeral Home.

"I know one thing for sure," Gibbons said. "Justin Bird saw the victim sooner after the murder than anybody else we know of, and that makes him important."

I give Oscar full points for the way he handled the situation that interrupted his Thursday night in front of ESPN. After putting out an all-points bulletin on Justin Bird, he'd briefly considered and rejected the idea of holding everybody in the theater. Instead, quickly sizing up the tremendous opportunity for making a bad situation worse, he had made sure the crime scene photos were taken as soon as possible and the body covered. As a result, a number of Erin citizens were shocked numb the next day when they found out from *The Erin Observer & News Ledger* that they'd walked by a dead body on their way to the parking lot after the otherwise-triumphant premier of *1895*. With the flashing light off, they might not have even noticed the police cars.

When I'd pointed out to Oscar that the cast and backstage crew of the play would take a while to get out of their costumes and makeup, he'd decided to go in and get Mac and Gibbons at the time I judged the play should be over. Lynda insisted on going along to be with Triple M when she got the news, so the three of us went in together.

Inside, I'd gone with Oscar as he rounded up Mac and Gibbons. "You will want to talk to the cast and backstage crew, of course," Mac said.

"Of course," Oscar agreed, clearly mystified. "And I'll ask them . . . ?"

"If they saw Justin leave, and if so which door did he go out. There was no way he could leave by the back door and approach Bill Kirtland without being seen by him, not while Kirtland was standing where he was shot."

I was listening to all this with half an ear as I watched Lynda. She stood in front of Sister Mary Margaret Malone, held her hands, broke the news to her. The expression of stunned shock on her face, followed by tears, broke my heart. She collapsed on Lynda.

Now, twenty minutes or so later, the tears were still flowing as Polly and Lynda walked over to the covered body. They stood for some time as if in quiet prayer. Then Triple M raised her right hand and made the sign of the cross. As they turned away, the good sister shook her head and I heard her say, "Oh, Justin, what have you done?"

Chapter Ten
Jealousy?

That was a good question, and I chewed over it half the night. Justin had practically signed a confession by running away. But Mac's pointed questions to Oscar had made it clear that Justin as the killer didn't make a lot of sense. Take motive, for example. What possible reason could Justin have for killing a man he didn't know? Kirtland had just come to town. The robbery theory seemed weak unless we found out that he was carrying a lot of money on him, which didn't seem likely. Even madmen have motives—mad ones. Around 3 A.M., I sent Lynda a text. *Lack of motive for Justin bugs me.* Only later that morning did I find out from Lynda herself that Oscar thought he had the motive covered.

His questioning at the Lyceum had been inconclusive. He hadn't found anybody on the cast or crew who'd paid attention to when or how Justin had left the building. That was no surprise. Justin was a non-entity to everybody but Triple M, who apparently had been concentrating on her job backstage.

Around 7:30 on Friday morning I called my parents, who are early risers, to assure them that I had nothing to do with the murder they would be learning about in the media. I even believed that at the time, but I don't think they did. I had a track record.

When I came down to breakfast I found the day's well-thumbed edition of *The Erin Observer & News-Ledger* face up on the table with the headline **ERIN VISITOR SHOT TO DEATH** showing. I'd already read the story on my iPhone. It carried the byline Bernard J. Silverstein, but I knew that it included a lot of uncredited contributions by Lynda Teal. Ben used to cover crime, along with about half a dozen other beats, before he succeeded Lynda as news editor of the paper. It was natural for him as a salaried employee to jump on the late-breaking story. Or maybe he just hadn't broken himself of the reporting habit yet.

The mood around the breakfast table, already occupied by George Apple and Amy Quong, was solemn as I pulled up a chair. "Morning," George murmured. I nodded at each of them.

Sally Apple came in with a pot of tea. "Isn't it just awful!" She nodded in the direction of the newspaper headline. "I knew something was wrong when the chief showed up backstage, but he just asked questions—he didn't answer any. Then somebody, I forget who, told me it looked like there was an accident out back. I never dreamed it was murder!"

"Hard to believe I talked to him just a few hours before it happened," George added. "He came back here at five o'clock or so with a bottle of Silk Stocking wine and asked where there was a good place to eat dinner. I recommended Bobbie McGee's." He shook his head. "Last time I saw him."

"You're lucky you didn't see him after he was shot," I said. "Unfortunately, I did."

"How awful for you!" Amy Quong exclaimed. There wasn't a hint of sarcasm in her tone. "What was that like? Never mind, I don't want to know. Tell me, do visitors to Erin get murdered often?" *Not more than once each, Ms. Quong.* Today she was wearing a grey pinstriped suit, but she'd added a bit of color with a scarlet silk scarf around her neck. Red was definitely her color. It occurred to me that she might be pretty if she smiled. And if I hadn't been an almost-married man, I might have tried to find out for sure when the circumstances were right.

"That depends on what you mean by often," I said. I'd never thought about it before, but each of Mac's other cases had also involved an out-of-towner. "Lately, it's been happening more than usual."

George Apple gave me a murderous look. I made a mental note that he had no sense of humor. "You don't have to worry about your safety," he assured Ms. Quong. "It says in the paper that the chief knows who did it."

"Well, he has a person of interest," I said.

Sally Apple set down a plate of quiche. "Yes, and it's that creepy Justin Bird. He ran away. Who else could it have been?"

"I have no idea," I admitted. "But there are a few things that don't add up for making the case against Justin." I related the questions that Mac posed to Oscar calling into question the logic of Justin-as-killer. "Granted, Gibbons thinks that the kid might have been able to approach Kirtland without being seen if he came out by the side door. But none of you crew members saw him leave that way."

"I'm not so sure," Sally said. "Now that I think about it, I'm not so sure I didn't." *That's what they call the power of suggestion.* "Oh, dear. We don't have any milk. George, you forgot to buy a new bottle last night."

"Anyway," I said, struggling manfully to keep the conversation on track, "the rest of Mac's points are valid, especially the lack of motive."

"Who is this Mac person?" Ms. Quong asked.

"Sebastian McCabe," Sally said. "He's a very smart man."

"Is he a policeman?"

"No, he's a professor," I said. "He's also a mystery writer and a magician."

She sipped her tea and raised her carefully penciled eyebrows at the same time, proving that she was coordinated. "Hmm. He sounds like an interesting one."

I nodded. "That he is."

"I would like to meet him." She was really breaking out of her shell this morning, talking much more than she had yesterday. "Perhaps he could solve the case of my missing earrings."

"Missing?" George repeated.

"They are very special, with many diamonds. I wanted to wear them out to dinner last night but they were not in my jewelry case."

"When did you last see them?" I said. This question has never proved helpful in thousands of years of asking it, but it seems to be imbedded in human DNA.

"I am not sure, but probably before my move from Illinois."

"Look again, dear," Sally said. "I'm sure they'll turn up. I misplace my jewelry all the time."

George started asking a bunch of police procedural-style questions about Oscar and his troops, like a *Law & Order* and *CSI* fan. How many cops did the chief bring in? Did anybody else hear the shot? Did the cops canvass the streets to try to find somebody who may have heard or seen anything? I was just about to point out that they only had three cops on the scene (see question number one) and probably would be using the news media to try to find witnesses when the sound of *Boléro* exploded in my pocket. It was my iPhone with a call from Lynda. The phone doesn't do *Boléro* for just anybody, only for my beloved.

"Excuse me," I said, standing up fast and moving toward the doorway out of the dining room. "It's my fiancée."

"She's got you well trained," George said with a wink and a nod. I half expected Amy Quong to whip a fourteen-inch knife out of her suit coat and yell, "Die, you sexist pig," but she didn't even blink. I'd forgotten for a minute that she works at Gamble Bank. Bankers are not noted for a sense of high drama.

"Good morning," I said into the phone.

"What's good about it?" Lynda snapped, her husky voice rife with tension. "My parents are in town, I haven't been able to get all the numbers I need to finish the budget for the new fiscal year—which was due a week ago, by the way—and Jacqui Daniel told me at Starbucks this morning that the baker for our wedding cake was sued last year by a disgruntled bride!"

She sounded like she needed a good scream, but that would hurt my ears. A workout at the gym would also be helpful, but that wasn't on her schedule this morning.

"How about a backrub?" I suggested.

"Now," she steamed on, ignoring my thoughtful offer, "I find out that Oscar thinks he knows the motive for Bill Kirtland's murder and it's terrible!"

"Come again?" *I know you're running on caffeine, my sweet, but at least slow down enough that I can jump on board.*

"Oscar's theory is built around jealousy. When he interviewed Polly last night to find out how well she knew Bill, she told him the truth—that he was an old flame she'd kept in touch with. Gibbons is convinced from the way he saw Justin Bird looking at Polly while they were working backstage that his feelings for her are, let's say, not fraternal." *You've been hanging around Mac too much; you're starting to sound like him.* "Oscar figures that Justin killed Kirtland so he could have Polly for himself."

I was barely used to the idea that a nun—sorry, religious sister—would have an ex-boyfriend. The idea that one would be at the center of a love triangle was a little jarring. On the other hand, Triple M is cute, full of enthusiastic energy, and one of the sweetest people on the planet. I could see, in theory, how a guy shot by Cupid's arrows might overlook a little thing like Sister Mary Margaret's Daughters of St. Augustine lapel pin. Sisters do occasionally leave that calling for marriage, just as priests do. Whether Justin ever had a chance with Triple M was beside the point as long as he thought he did.

So I had to admit that jealousy was a credible motive— never mind the unpleasant memory of the time my own reputation for jealousy of Lynda had made *me* a murder suspect.

Just because it wasn't true then, that didn't mean it couldn't be true now.

"Well," Lynda prodded as I was running all this through my mental calculator, "what are you thinking? I can almost hear the wheels turning."

"I'm not saying I buy it, but it's not totally crazy. How do you know all this about Gibbons and Oscar, by the way?"

"I may be out of the newsroom, but I'm not so far away from it." That's literally true. Lynda's offices are in *The Erin Observer & News-Ledger* building, although she travels a lot visiting other outposts of the Grier Ohio NewsGroup. "Oscar told Johanna Rawls this morning. She's posting a story on *The Observer*'s website now."

The chief had been busy. So had Johanna, the ambitious young journalist who had taken Ben Silverstein's place in the reportorial ranks. I called her "Tall Rawls" because she was a woman I could look up to when she wore high heels. Oscar hates dealing with the press, but he must have been eager to talk about what he viewed as a triumph. Or maybe Johanna had charmed it out of him. He was more susceptible to that approach than he would ever admit.

"And why is this so terrible?" I asked. Identifying Kirtland's murderer, dealing with him, and moving on sounded like a positive to me.

"Because Polly is spazzing out, that's why." I appreciated Lynda's restraint in not adding "you idiot," which is clearly what she was thinking. "This is a nightmare for her on so many levels. Somebody she cared deeply about has been murdered and another friend is the only suspect. She's been trying to save Justin Bird, so she hopes it's not true that he did it. If he did do it, it means that she's failed in her mission. And if he did it because he's smitten with her, then she feels doubly responsible."

"Oh." How the hell was I supposed to figure all *that* out? I could barely follow it once it was explained to me.

"You have to do something!"

Why me, dear? And do what? The kid is probably as guilty as a fox caught in a henhouse with a mouthful of feathers. "Do something? Okay, right. Well, tell Polly not to worry about a thing. I'll talk to Mac. He wasn't buying Oscar's scenario for the murder last night. I'm sure he'll have some ideas."

Mac always has ideas. More often than not they get me in trouble, but this was no time to worry about that. Maybe I should have.

Chapter Eleven
"Jefferson, We're Needed"

Aneliese Pokorny brought a cup of decaf into my office and sat it on my desk. Then she sat herself in the chair across from me.

"Well, you had a large day yesterday."

Translation: Give me all the gory details right now. Popcorn had sat with Kate in the audience, and like the rest of the audience hadn't a clue until later what had happened.

"Was that just one day?" I said.

A mostly-sleepless night tends to throw off your sense of timing. Plus, in less than forty-eight hours I had met both of Lynda's parents, moved out of my apartment, and seen the bleeding body of a man with whom I had eaten breakfast.

Quickly, I brought my irreplaceable administrative assistant up to date, all the way up to Lynda's phone call.

"So what's Mac going to do?" she asked.

Mac, Mac, Mac. Why does everybody think Mac is the only one who can solve a problem? And that includes me!

"I haven't approached him yet," I said. "I thought it might be nice of me to actually make a few perfunctory steps toward justifying my salary this morning first. What's going on with Wendy Nichols?"

Wendy was our latest communications crisis. A star center for the St. Benignus Lady Dragons, she had drawn the wrong kind of attention to our women's basketball program by shoplifting at a Victoria's Secret in a suburban Cincinnati mall. On the day the story broke, Popcorn had insisted on reading

me the embarrassing list of intimate apparel stolen, claiming
that she liked to see my face turn the color of my hair.

"The judge gave her a small fine, no community
service."

That was about what I'd expected. If anything really
important had happened while I was out of the office yesterday
I would have received e-mails, texts, tweets, and phone calls
from Popcorn, the media, alumni, and Ralph Pendergast, my
insufferable boss.

"What else is going on?" I asked, kind of hoping I'd be
needed for something.

As Popcorn started to brief me on the promotional
YouTube video being put together for us by a local high school
kid, my iPhone made that incoming sound. I had a text
message. I pulled out the phone and read:

Jefferson, we're needed.

"What is it?" Popcorn asked.

"It's just Mac with a lame riff on *The Avengers*, circa
1966. You know, John Steed, Mrs. Peel. Apparently I'm Mrs.
Peel."

I texted him back, initiating a text-message dialogue.

JEFF: What do you mean "we"?

MAC: I am lost without my Watson!

He was mixing cultural metaphors in a single text
exchange, but that wasn't what bothered me. Best friend and
brother-in-law or not, I hate it when he assumes I'm always at
his beck and call, ready to take my place as his second banana
at the drop of a deerstalker hat.

But I needed a favor from him. If I was going to keep
my fiancée happy, which was the most important thing in the
world to me, then I would have to ask him to look into the
Justin Bird business.

JEFF: OK, what's up?

*MAC: Sr. Mary Margaret is seeking our help for Justin. Please
meet me at Campus Ministries pronto.*

I guess this was my day to kill the proverbial two fowls with a single projectile.

Chapter Twelve
The Spy Who Loved Her

Campus Ministries is on the other side of the grounds from my office in Carey Hall, but I'm a fast walker. I got there in about five minutes to find Mac already filling most of Triple M's modest office. Her walls are covered with inspiring posters, the bookcases crammed with works of theology, spirituality, and science fiction.

Triple M was there, too, of course, dressed in a denim jumper over a white mock turtleneck shirt. Her youthfulness had taken a hike since yesterday. She looked all of her mid-thirties and then some, her lack of makeup doing her no favors. Judging by the bags under her eyes and the sleepiness in them, she'd been awake last night as much as I had. We must have been a pretty pair.

"Thanks for coming, Jeff."

"Yeah, sure."

She stood on the tiptoes of her gym shoes and gave me a sisterly hug.

Mac pulled a cigar from the breast pocket of his sport coat. He couldn't smoke it here, but nobody would stop him from chewing on it. "As you may have surmised, Jefferson, I have already committed my available energies, with your help, to look into the murder of Bill Kirtland. Polly understands that I am seeking the truth, which may not necessarily help Justin Bird."

"But I'm sure it will," Polly said. This optimism, so typical of her, had no basis in fact that I could discern. *Polly must be short for Pollyanna.*

"Let us hope so, Polly. I want to start by making sure you understand that you are uniquely important to this case—I might call you the hinge person—because you knew both the victim and Oscar's 'person of interest.' The fact that you also have been speculated as the motive for the murder adds greatly to that importance."

"But that's just bullshit, Mac!"

Salty language was not a staple in Triple M's vocabulary, but it wasn't unknown either. I'd been around once when she'd stubbed her toe. On that occasion her Army background had become quickly apparent.

"I note that your position is clear," Mac said dryly. "Nevertheless, any effort on our part to uncover the truth must begin right now with a rather intense debriefing. I assume that you are free to talk at some length?"

"Yes. I don't have any commitments until a staff meeting with Father Juan this afternoon. Sit down."

"Good." The chairs were wide enough for Mac and comfortable enough for a student discussing spiritual matters. "I will ask you some questions that I think might be helpful. Jefferson will jump in as he feels the need. We will begin with the victim. First, I will summarize what I think we know about Bill Kirtland and you will verify or correct based on your knowledge."

That didn't take long: Bill Kirtland lived in Louisville, called himself a security consultant—"perhaps a purposefully vague description," Mac said ominously—and was passing through Erin on some undefined business.

"I don't know anything about his business," Triple M said. "He wrote to me on Thursday morning, through Facebook, to say that he had sudden business in Ohio and he'd like to see me if I were available on Friday."

"You were in regular Facebook contact?"

She nodded. "I use it a lot, Bill not so much. He sent me a Friend invitation, I don't know, maybe a little over a year ago. I had to think about it a little bit, whether it was a good thing to stir up those memories and emotions. I finally decided they'd always be there anyway, and besides, I'm a sister, not hermit."

"Memories and emotions," Mac repeated, rolling the unlit cigar between his thumb and fingers. "I gather you were rather close at one time."

Sister Mary Margaret shifted in her seat. She ran a hand through her short, black hair in a nervous gesture.

"We dated for more than two years, closer to three. I'd met Bill right after the end of a disastrous relationship—my fiancé got another woman pregnant. So I didn't plan on getting real serious real fast. After a couple of years, though, Bill asked me to marry him. I didn't say no right away, but eventually I had to. I wasn't opposed to marriage in principle, despite my horrendous experience, and I loved Bill. But it just didn't seem right for me. I was starting to experience these spiritual yearnings, so I decided to leave the Army and see where that led me." She gestured around the room. "This is where it led me. It's a good life."

I wanted to hug her, but that would have been awkward with the desk between us. Instead, I tried to lower the emotional temperature in the room a little bit by shifting the subject.

"What did you do in the Army?" I'd always been curious but never got around to asking.

"Bill and I were both 97 Bravo. That's the MOS—Military Occupational Specialty—for enlisted personnel who work in counter-intelligence."

Mac raised an eyebrow. "In common parlance, you were spies."

Sister 007?

"No, we were counterspies."

Oh, that's completely different.

This news may have been just a juicy tidbit to Mac, but I was seeing something else. "That sounds like a job rife with potential murder motives," I said, somewhat thoughtlessly given that Triple M had labored in the same vineyard.

She shook her head. "It sounds more dramatic than it was. Bill and I were just little cogs in a very big wheel. We worked with the Army and NATO in Brussels—that's where we met—mostly doing background investigations of personnel and briefings on SAEDA and port security."

"What's that in English?" I asked.

"Subversion and Espionage Directed Against the Army. Our briefings covered anti-terrorism security measures."

"That was all?" If Mac was trying to hide his disappointment, he failed utterly.

"That was the routine part. We also handled the initial investigations of suspected terrorist activity. We turned over our findings to the CIA for follow-up."

"I am sure your work was very important," Mac said, "but that was some time ago and many other individuals did the same work before and since. Of course, one could spin a theory involving some information that Bill acquired during one of those initial investigations—"

"It's not like he would be the only one involved," Triple M said. "I don't think he could have found out something, kept it to himself, and used it in a blackmail plot or something like that."

"Very well," Mac said. "Let us move on. Bill identified himself to Jeff yesterday morning as a 'security consultant.' That strikes me as a rather elastic term, perhaps deliberately so. It could mean anything. Do you know more precisely the nature of his work?"

She thought a minute. "I don't think that ever came up on Facebook, and I know we didn't talk about it when he was here."

"What did you talk about, might I ask?"

"We talked about *my* work. He met me here in the office around ten o'clock. I showed him around, explained what we do in campus ministry. I told him a little about my volunteer work at the jail." She bit her lip, and then added with difficulty: "He wanted to know if I was happy with the Daughters of St. Augustine and I told him I'm very happy."

"What do you think would have happened if you had answered differently?" Mac said.

"I'm not sure. But the way he asked the question, I don't think he was surprised by my answer. It was like he was asking me just to be sure. Excuse me, Mac, but what do these questions have to do with the murder? I really don't mind answering, we're friends, but I'm just not sure where you're going with this."

Mac sighed. "Perhaps nowhere. I am trying to establish whether Bill was really here only to see you or whether he had some other, secret purpose as well—perhaps to meet someone who had a hand in his death. I presume that, to the best of your knowledge, he knew no one else in Erin?"

"I'm sure that he didn't. Not unless he was deliberately hiding it from me."

"What did he do here in Erin on the last day of his life?" Mac asked. "Perhaps that will be indicative of something."

"Well, as I said, he met me here in the morning. That was around ten o'clock. Bill asked me to meet him for dinner, but I told him I had to be at the theater by six. Dinner sounded a little too serious to me, anyway, but I was free for lunch. We met at Daniel's. I thought he would like the retro menu and décor."

Daniel's Apothecary, with a real soda fountain and a menu to delight James Dean, is right next to *The Erin Observer & News-Ledger*. I've lunched there dozens of times with Lynda, once in a while with Triple M tagging along.

"What time was that?"

"Maybe twelve-fifteen or so. I was running a little late coming out of a meeting."

"Did he tell you what he'd done since leaving here?"

"When I came in he mentioned that he'd just got there. He said he's been antiquing at Garrison's." One of a number of antique stores on Main and nearby streets, Garrison's is just on the other side of Daniel's.

"Did he act strange in any way?"

Give Triple M full points for stopping to think about it. But she finally shook her head, bouncing her short hair. "No, not at all. I'm sure of it."

"I assume from what you said earlier that he didn't seem to know anyone else in the restaurant."

"No."

"Did you talk to anyone else?"

"I waved to a few people but didn't say more than hi. I didn't introduce Bill to anybody."

Bad move, Sister Mary Margaret. If you're a sister or a priest or a married person out in public with a member of the opposite sex, you should introduce your friend to everybody in sight. People have such suspicious minds—people like me, anyway.

I thought it was about time I got in a question, so I anticipated Mac: "Did he say anything about how he was going to spend the rest of his day?"

A nod. "He told me he was coming to the play because I was working backstage." Her voice choked at the end. She stopped and swallowed before going on. "He asked me what else there was to do in Erin. I mentioned Pages Gone By, because he always loved old books, and the Farmers Market on Court Street. And I told him the Silk Stocking Winery is kind of fun if he was willing to drive a little ways out of town."

Pages Gone By was a used book store. I had a friend of the female persuasion who worked there.

"Do you have a picture of Bill?" Mac asked.

"Not a new one. You might try running a search on Google Images." I'd have thought of that, eventually. Triple M is very savvy about using technology.

She put her hand up to cover a mammoth yawn. "Sorry. I'm sleep deprived." *You and me both, Sister.* "I need coffee. Do you want some? We only have high-test." I said no, but Mac never turned down anything bad for him. Triple M got up from her desk and disappeared into a kitchenette around the corner. I looked at Mac, sitting in silence like a Buddha, and wondered what was going on inside his big head. I might have asked if Triple M hadn't returned quickly, carrying an Amazon.com travel mug for herself and a Star Trek mug for Mac.

Mac blew on his and sipped. "Tell us about Justin Bird."

"Okay." Triple M took a healthy slug of coffee-flavored caffeine. "He's smart enough to make something out of himself but he keeps making bad choices, like dropping out of high school in his senior year. I keep trying to get him to get his GED. There's nothing wrong with working at Burger Castle, it's honest work, but I think he could do better. He's twenty-three years old and everybody thinks of him as a kid because he acts like a kid. I keep telling him it's time to grow up."

"Ouch," I said.

"Somebody needs to give him the bad news, and his parents weren't getting the job done. So that's Justin in a nutshell—immature and unambitious. But he's also kind of sweet. I can't believe that he would deliberately hurt anybody."

"Wait a minute," I interjected. "One of his bad choices was shooting up a school bus!"

"Don't forget it was empty at the time. He was being childish. His girlfriend dumped him for a school bus driver and that was his idea of revenge. He doesn't even know anything about guns—he took his mother's boyfriend's .22 without permission. If his target had been any smaller than a bus he probably would have missed."

"That little episode landed him in Oscar's lockup?" Mac said.

"Right. That's where we met. I think it was about two months ago. He didn't show much interest in praying with me, but he did want somebody to talk to. He was very scared. But since it was a first offense he got off with a fine and community service. I arranged it that his community service is helping me here on campus. I'm trying to help him at the same time."

"Why do you think he ran last night?"

"Isn't that obvious? He's not some hardened criminal, he's really afraid of the law. And because he'd been in trouble before, he was sure that Oscar would suspect him. I told you he wasn't stupid—but he made another bad choice by running. "

"And I assume you don't know where he is?"

She shook her head. "I keep hoping he'll call me and I can try to talk him into turning himself in."

"Is there anybody else he might turn to—family or friends?"

"He's mentioned some other friends from time to time, but all I got were first names—Logan and Sam, I think. His family is a train wreck, every cliché of a bad situation you can think of. His father is out of the picture and his mother is an alcoholic with a long stream of abusive live-in boyfriends."

Mac drank his coffee, as if to buck himself up. "Polly, you have pooh-poohed the notion that Justin might have shot Bill out of jealousy." *She called it bullshit; yeah, I guess that's pooh-pooh.* "Why is that unthinkable? You are an attractive woman, if I may say so, and Justin was a male who was spending a lot of time with you. It is not unnatural that he had come to feel an attraction for you."

"Oh, he had a crush on me, all right. A girl can tell. But I told him if he made one false move I'd give him his first taekwondo lesson, and I made sure he knew I wasn't joking. So how would killing Bill change anything?"

In my head I could hear Oscar telling Mac, "You're being too rational." Somebody who kills out of jealousy most likely isn't calculating the outcome logically.

"Putting that to one side, did Justin know about Bill?"

"Well, yes." She seemed to respond with reluctance. "Bill walked me over to the theater after lunch. There was some last-minute stuff to do on the set before opening night, so I arranged to work just a half-day here yesterday. Justin was already at the Lyceum when we arrived. I introduced Bill to him as an old friend." She swallowed. "Bill said something like, 'Actually, we dated for almost three of the best years of my life.' And then he kissed me and said goodbye. That was the last time I saw him."

Chapter Thirteen
Game Plan

Mac and I walked back across campus together in silence at first. While Mac lit a cigar, my fatigued brain shot off in weird directions. *Why was it so hard to believe that Triple M was a spy? James Bond's boss was an M—and a woman, when played by Judi Dench. But M in 1895 was played by Mac, who could never be a . . .*

"Well, Jefferson," Mac broke in on my disordered thoughts, "what did you make of all that?"

"All that" didn't amount to much. We'd learned that Triple M and Bill Kirtland had both worked in U.S. Army counterintelligence, but the person most eager to believe that someone other than Justin Bird had killed Bill—Sister Polly herself—didn't see a motive there. It appeared certain that Bill knew no one in town other than Triple M. On the flip side, it was pretty clear that he still had romantic feelings for the good sister—and so did Justin.

"Poor Polly," I said. "If there was a 'Get Out of Jail Free' card for Justin Bird in anything she said, I sure missed it. It's sweet that Polly's so sure he's innocent, but she thinks the best of everybody, even politicians and telephone solicitors. I think a guy who'd shoot up a school bus just because his ex-honey's new boyfriend is a bus driver might be exactly the kind of wacko to kill somebody over a woman he could never have anyway."

Mac thoughtfully blew cigar smoke away from me. "Am I to believe that Justin committed murder on the basis of one brief meeting with his future victim? And with such presence of mind that he procured a silencer first?"

"Stranger things have happened. In fact, we've *seen* stranger things happen. What's your theory?"

"'It is a capital mistake to theorize before one has data.'—Sherlock Holmes, 'A Scandal in Bohemia.' We need more data, old boy."

"Like what? I'm afraid I already know more about Polly than I really wanted to know."

"Not about Bill, however," Mac countered. "I particularly want to know how he spent the last day of his life. We shall need to do some legwork."

Before I had a chance to find out what he meant by that, Mac's smart phone erupted into *Ride of the Valkyries,* his ring tone. He looked at the screen. "Blast it—it's Figg. I suppose I had better answer." He touched the screen and put the phone up to his ear. "Yes?"

For the next few minutes I was subjected to the always-annoying (and increasingly more frequent) experience of hearing one end of a cell phone conversation.

"What? That is nonsense! What sort of changes? You know full well that ending is authentic, Figg! Kindly try not to be absurd. The audience loved it and the Henry Knox Wilcox review in this morning's newspaper was quite enthusiastic by his rather dour standards. Well, if you insist on doing so I can hardly be expected to perform in the mishmash that results. You would not dare! Well, I thought I knew you, Figg, but it appears that I was wrong. Your ethical standards are even lower than I thought. Very well, then, I shall see what I can do with the script."

He disconnected in a huff and put away the phone. "That man has an incredibly inflated ego!" *Hello Kettle? This is Pot. You're black!*

"So what did old Mutton-Chops want?"

"He decided overnight that the ending of *1895* falls flat. Apparently the Holmes brothers saving the empire and Holmes being called to Windsor to receive an emerald tiepin from his grateful queen is not dramatic enough! He had the nerve to demand rewrites—for tonight's performance!"

"Is that such a big deal? You're a fast writer. You knocked out a book in a month once, not that it was any good."

He favored me with a sour look. "I do not work well under outside pressure."

"Then tell Figg to write it himself."

"He suggested that, knowing full well that he could scarcely write the directions to his own home. You heard me say that in that event I could not perform. He threatened to replace me with my understudy."

"Who's your understudy?"

"He is, blast him!"

"Oh. Then I guess you'd better get to work."

"Indeed. I am highly fortunate to have you to make the necessary inquiries today."

"Me!" This wasn't going at all well, although it did have the virtue of familiarity. We'd been down this road "What makes you think I'm going to do that?" *Other than the fact that I've always done it before.* "You're not the only one with a life. I have a day job, you know, with an office in Carey Hall and everything."

My brother-in-law, smoking serenely, ignored my finely honed sarcasm. "I simply haven't the time to be retracing Bill Kirtland's steps. Ergo, I must rely on you. Surely it is obvious that you are much more suited to the task than I am anyway? You are gumshoe material. I am Mycroft Holmes." He seemed suddenly struck by his own declaration. "Yes, I am Mycroft Holmes! You provide the data and I will provide the enlightenment!"

Oh, brother! Hey, I wonder if Sherlock Holmes ever said that?

"No way," I snapped. Impressed though I was that he actually managed to work the word "ergo" into a conversation, I was still miffed. "This is a wild goose chase and you know it. Why should—"

Incoming! A text message had just arrived. Since I sometimes get texts from the media, and therefore this could actually be work-related, I interrupted myself and pulled out my iPhone. The message was from Lynda:

Tnx for helping mmm. U r my hero.

I wrote back:

I try.

So much for my protests. I'd feel like a heel now if I didn't do what my beloved had just thanked me for doing.

"Never mind whatever I thought I wanted to say," I told Mac, trying to keep the sigh out of my voice as I put the phone back in my pocket. "What's the first move?"

By this time we were outside Herbert Hall, at the far end of the quadrangle, where his office is located. "It would be helpful to construct a written timetable of Bill Kirtland's last day, which we can add to as we get more information. Come with me."

The dragon at the gate was in residence—Heidi Guildenstern, administrative assistant for the popular culture program that Mac directs. She sits right outside his inner office. The proper Ms. Guildenstern, a forty-year employee of St. Benignus, regards both Mac and the program with ill-concealed disdain. She herself could be a 97 Bravo, or whatever they called the people who were spies rather than counterspies. I had long suspected that she occasionally passed on bits of harmful information to Ralph Pendergast, the college provost and our *bête noir*, as Mac likes to call him. Thank goodness that St. Benignus wasn't involved in this murder, meaning that I wouldn't have to endure a new series of Ralph rampages.

"Good morning, Professor McCabe, Mr. Cody," Heidi said, dragging her washed-out grey eyes from her computer to

greet us with stiff courtesy. I don't know what she found so
fascinating on that screen, but I would bet it wasn't video
games.

"Morning, Heidi." Mac steamed passed her. I waved
cheerfully. She glared. *I like you, too, Grendel.*

Mac's office is a nightmare of books and papers. I don't
know how he finds the desk, much less anything specific on it.
But somehow he stuck his hand into a paper pile and came out
with a yellow 8½ by 11-inch pad. He began to write in his
precise handwriting. After a minute or two he handed it over to
me, with the comment, "This includes a few tentative
assumptions that are indicated by question marks. We cannot
be sure, for example, that Bill Kirtland actually visited Pages
Gone By as Polly suggested—that awaits your confirmation."

I read:

Timetable—Bill Kirtland's Last Day

8:00 A.M.	*Breakfast at Shamrocks & Ivy*
10:00 A.M.	*Polly's office*
11:00 A.M.	*Garrison's*
12:30 P.M.	*Daniel's with Polly*
1:30 P.M.	*Pages Gone By?*
?	*Farmer's Market?*
Before 5 P.M.	*Silk Stocking Winery*
Approx. 5 P.M.	*Shamrocks & Ivy*
After 5 P.M.	*Bobbie McGee's?*
8:00 P.M.	*Lyceum Theater*

"That leaves a lot of time unaccounted for," I noted.

Mac nodded. "That is where the legwork comes in. In
the process of asking questions at the places where we know he
went, and where we think he went, you may be able to fill in
more of the timetable. In addition, the contents of his pockets,
which we can ascertain from Oscar, may prove helpful."

"How so?"

"They may contain brochures, receipts, perhaps some small items that he purchased." Mac glanced at his Sherlock Holmes wristwatch. *Shouldn't you have a Mycroft Holmes pocket watch?* "I believe I can spare a half-hour, perhaps an hour, to drop in on Oscar and ask about the contents of Bill's pockets, as well as a few other questions I have in mind."

I was about to ask Mac whether he was sure that wouldn't overburden him when the sound of *Boléro* came out of my pocket.

"Yes, my sweet?" I said sweetly.

"Get over here right now, Jeff." My strong fiancée sounded beyond stressed this time—on the verge of tears. I felt a sudden panic.

"What's the matter? Where are you? Are you hurt?'

"I'm in my office and I'm not hurt—but my mother's going to be if you don't get over here and stop me. She's trying to ruin our wedding!"

Chapter Fourteen
Mother-of-the-Bridezilla

Mac and I agreed to meet at the jail as soon as I could extricate myself from this wedding crisis. I rushed across campus, grabbed my bike, and pedaled like mad the few blocks to downtown Erin and *The Erin Observer & News-Ledger.*

Even if I hadn't been alert for it I would have known something was going on as soon as I walked in. All eyes in the small newsroom were focused on the big glass office that Lynda had inherited from Frank Woodford, the editor and general manager, when she'd moved up to the corporate job with the parent company.

By all eyes I mean Frank himself, who had ventured into the newsroom from his new office for a good look; Benjamin J. Silverstein, Lynda's successor as news editor; Maggie Barton, about seventy years old and never missed a day of work until that skydiving accident last fall; and Johanna "Tall" Rawls, whom I made a mental note to see before I left the building. That was most of the non-business staff, except for freelancers like that pompous Henry Knox Wilcox, the drama critic.

They were looking at Lynda and Lucia, facing off at opposite ends of the rectangular office like a couple of boxers in a grudge match. They were yelling at each other in loud Italian (*"Diavoli d'inferno!" "Maledizione!"*), and their hands were moving like the arms of windmills. It was fascinating, but so was a car wreck. *So I'm supposed to walk into this and do something to make Lynda happy? Nice job. I never knew weddings could be so dangerous.*

And yet, it would be hard for any red-blooded American male like me not to enjoy looking at the two womanly women. Lynda was taller, younger, and not as jaw-dropping gorgeous as Lucia, but the family resemblance to her mother was easy to see in their shared oval faces, dark complexions, honey blond hair (somewhat suspiciously blond in Lucia's case), and statuesque figures. Lynda, whose hair was curlier, was dressed for business in a white blouse, a plaid dress, and big loop earrings of gold. She looked like a Scottish lass. *Hoot, mon!* Her mother wore khaki slacks and a frilly black satin blouse with a plunging neckline. The outfit was low-key, although I'm sure the label said Dior or Gucci, but it was accented with more diamonds than a deck of playing cards.

I took a deep breath and marched into Lynda's office.

"Jeff, darling! Thank God you came!"

That was Lucia, but I could tell from Lynda's eyes that she would have said something similar if her mother hadn't beat her to the punch.

"So," I said, "how's everything going?"

Perhaps that was not quite the right question to ask. But I'm not really sure. They both responded quickly and forcefully, resulting in a cacophony of mixed English and Italian. I wish I'd had a referee whistle to blow.

I yelled above the tumult. "What seems to be the problem here?" *Jeez, Jeff, what a cliché. Is that the best you can do?*

Lynda, clearly on the verge of tears, picked up her satin and lace wedding dress, which I hadn't noticed hanging on a clothes tree in the corner. "You've seen this dress, Jeff. It's tasteful, it's beautiful. She wants cleavage. I don't want my boobs hanging out on the altar in front of God and everybody during our wedding!"

No surprise there. Lynda's Victorian modesty always was one of her charms, up to a point. (After that, it was frustrating.)

Lucia clucked and rolled her eyes in a way so like Lynda it was uncanny. "Don't be so silly, *carissma*. God made your boobs—He just made them too small."

That's an outright lie, you jealous battleaxe! I happen to know that Lynda's measurements after a month at the gym are an aesthetically pleasing 38-28-38. An hourglass would envy that figure. And it's all natural. So is her nose!

My strong desire to spring to Lynda's defense was hampered by my inability to figure out how to do it. "Her boobs are quite big enough, thank you very much!" just didn't seem like the right thing to say to my future mother-in-law. Nor could I see Lynda applauding that particular rejoinder.

That's what I was thinking when I suddenly realized that Lucia was still talking and had moved on to other areas of her displeasure with the wedding plans. Worse yet, she was talking to me, as if looking for an ally.

". . . outside in a park, *ad esempio*, I mean if you absolutely *couldn't* have the wedding in Barbados. A park or botanical garden would be lovely at this time of the year, with flowers and trees in bloom. Much nicer than some stuffy old church. Don't you think so, Jeff?"

She fixed me with her wide brown eyes and fluttered her long lashes.

"Um," I said, after a thoughtful pause.

That church, St. Edward the Confessor, and its pastor, Fr. Peter Nguyen, mean a lot to Lynda. But perhaps she thought her mother couldn't understand. Instead of playing defense, she went on the offense.

"Mother is an expert on weddings," she said between clenched teeth. "She's had so many."

That was a low blow—calling Lucia "Mother." But Lucia ignored it and continued her rant.

"Your wedding planner really should be shot or deported, *carina*, whichever would be more painful. Thank goodness that I am here to rescue this disaster!"

"We didn't have a wedding planner." Lynda was raising her voice again. "Jeff and I did this all by ourselves."

Well, really, I had very little to do with it. But I'm totally on board with everything!

The color slowly drained from Lucia's face as she processed this horrifying new bit of information. No wedding planner? *Non è possibile!*

I really wanted to be on Mac's wild goose chase. I'd rather visit every single business in downtown Erin asking about Bill Kirtland than be here right now. But I had to help Lynda. I saw right away that there was only one way to get her mother's mind off of her critique of our wedding plans: flirt. I put my arm around Lucia.

"You know why I'm looking forward to the wedding, Lucia?"

She trained those big baby browns on me and fluttered her false eyelashes. "I cannot imagine, darling. Truly I cannot."

"Because then we can dance and I'll have you all to myself."

Behind her mother's back, Lynda stuck a finger in her throat and pantomimed a gagging gesture. I thought that was a little much. She didn't seem to appreciate the work I was doing on her behalf. *Hey, it's not like I'm having any fun here getting up-close and personal with one of the world's most beautiful and famous women. I'm just doing this for you, Lyn, taking one for the team.*

"You naughty boy. What would Lynda say?" Lucia talked as if her daughter weren't half a room away. "She has always been so jealous of me."

Lynda's eyes popped. She opened her mouth as if to say something. I quickly beat her to it.

"About that dress, it doesn't really matter, you know," I told Lucia. "I mean, no one will even notice it. All eyes will be on you." I rubbed my chin thoughtfully. "Of course, if the neckline is low enough, people *might* pay attention to Lynda."

Lucia looked at the dress. "You know, it is rather pretty, for an off-the-rack dress." Lynda had sewn the dress herself, and it had taken her weeks. "You are a very clever man, Jeff, as well as handsome." She stepped closer into my personal space and the smell of her perfume—*Birth of Venus, I presume?*—was beyond intoxicating. No doubt about it: It should have been illegal in all fifty states, plus Guam, Puerto Rico and the U.S. Virgin Islands. My knees were getting weak. "Perhaps we should have lunch," Lucia suggested.

"Well, it's a little early for that." I chuckled. "And I have a lot to do. In fact, I should be going."

"I'm sorry to hear that," Lynda said. "I'll show you out."

She took my arm—rather possessively, but I didn't mind—and led me out of her office. All around the newsroom reporters and editors suddenly looked busier than I'd ever seen them, carefully looking anywhere but in our direction.

"You were marvelous, *tesoro mio*," Lynda whispered throatily. "The way you pretended to be under her thrall just like every other man was so convincing. Who knew you were such a good actor?"

Not bothering to try to figure out whether that was sarcasm or irony, I hastened to point out, "The important thing is that I got her off the dress. Crisis averted!"

"Until her next explosion," Lynda said gloomily. This did not seem the time to point out that her mother had not been the only one exploding. "So how's Mac going to save Justin?"

"Oh, he has a brilliant plan: Have Jeff do all the real work." I explained how Mac had dumped the legwork on me and I was supposed to meet him at Oscar's office as soon as I finished up my rescue operation here.

"You'd better get to it, then. Good luck." She gave me the public version of a fiancée's kiss, which took a while even though it was G-rated. I really didn't want it to end, to tell you the truth. We disentangled our arms with reluctance and Lynda marched—I think it's fair to call it that—back into her office. I wondered if she'd ever thought of having privacy drapes installed.

Halfway to the front door, now partially recovered from the double dose of Lynda and Lucia, I remembered an idea I'd had on the way in. I detoured over to Johanna Rawls's desk.

"Oh, hi, Jeff," she said, looking up from her computer. "How are wedding plans going?"

"Swell! Just great!" *Smooth as sandpaper.*

She stood up. In the short skirt she was wearing, her legs seemed to never end. Johanna is a Nordic type, slim with long, straight, light blond hair and fair skin. Today she was wearing a turtle-neck sweater hugging her curves. Not that I noticed.

"You know, I respect Ms. Teal so much," she said. "She's my role model."

"Well, you couldn't pick a better one," I said truthfully. I don't know why that made me feel proud, but it did. "Lynda tells me that you went to high school with Justin Bird."

"Yeah. Of course, he dropped out. That was—wow—about five years ago."

"What was he like?"

She thought. "He didn't really stand out. I guess he was what you'd call socially awkward. Seems to me he liked music, always had the ear buds in. But I didn't know him well, he wasn't a friend."

"Did it surprise you when he shot up that school bus?"

"I hadn't thought about him in years, so I don't know if you'd say it surprised me. Word on the street is that he was hammered at the time—from drinking like three beers. They say he's not much into drinking."

As I'd hoped, she knew more about Justin than she'd put into her story.

"You have friends in common?"

"Well, sure. This is Erin and we're about the same age. I'm friends with a few classmates who probably hang around with him—nodding-on-the street friends, I mean, not let's-go-out-for-drinks friends."

"That might be enough for what I'm thinking," I said. "You ought to try to get word to Justin that he should call his real friend, Sr. Mary Margaret Malone, and make arrangements to turn himself in. That would really be the best thing for him. Do you think you can do that?"

"I can sure try," she said quickly. "Maybe he'd be willing to give me an exclusive interview before he goes to the police, especially if he remembers me."

"I hope so. Just remember, I'd like to talk with him, too."

Chapter Fifteen
Jailhouse Talk

"So I hear your future mother-in-law's being a problem," Oscar said, looking a bit smug behind his green desk.

"Nothing I can't handle," I said, not to be outdone in smugness. Oscar looked disbelieving.

Mac had arrived before me at Oscar's office in the basement of City Hall, where the city jail is also located. I was slightly out of breath from the effort to join them. But judging by Oscar's opening conversational gambit, they must have spent their time gossiping about my wedding woes instead of discussing the murder of Bill Kirtland.

"Maybe that's one of the reasons I never got hitched," Oscar said. "I sure don't need some old hag complicating my life."

"Yeah," I said. "Hag." *Actually, Lucia's more like a veela, one of those supernatural seductresses in that Harry Potter movie.*

Mac raised an eyebrow at me, as if to say, "Wow, did he get a wrong number!" The chief, not seeing this, leaned back in his chair and folded his hands over his paunch. With that Panama hat on, he looked like the emperor of ice cream.

"By the way, anybody feel like talking about the murder?" I said, a little nettled that I'd rushed over here on my bike to find Oscar looking so cocksure and comfortable while Mac seemed bemused.

"I assure you that we already have," Mac said. "Oscar remains steadfast in his conviction that Justin is guilty."

Oscar put up his hands, as if in protest. "You have a good history, Mac. I'd be foolish not to listen to any other possibilities you want to give me. But so far all you've given me are objections. They're good ones, but they don't trump the fact that a kid with a record of gun violence and a motive to kill the victim (a) was with the dead body before anybody else and (b) fled the scene."

"Do you have an eyewitness?" Mac asked.

Oscar sat up. "Don't play games. You know I don't. How many murderers do it in front of an audience?"

"How many murderers phone 911 afterward?"

That smug look stole back over Oscar's face. "Lots of them, my friend. I've known a few myself. Some of them confessed when they phoned it in, some of them thought they'd deflect suspicion from themselves by reporting the murder."

"And did any of them then bolt as soon as the police arrived?" Mac fired back.

"None of them was Justin Bird." Oscar reached behind him for the pot of coffee always there and poured himself a cup. Why people who are already stressed will dose themselves with caffeine puzzles me.

"You do realize that Polly Malone doesn't buy your belief that she's the murder motive," I said.

"What nun would?" Oscar said. He slurped his coffee. "I mean, it's gotta be a little embarrassing, even if she didn't do anything to encourage Justin. And I'm sure she didn't. Besides, who wants to believe that somebody got killed because of you?" He lowered his voice as if sharing a secret. "I actually like Sister Polly. She thinks I don't because—well, I don't throw out the welcome mat for her. That's just the way I am with do-gooders who come into my jail and make nice with my guests. But I like her. She cheers this place up. I'm sorry she got caught up in this mess."

"You find a lot of significance in Justin's previous record of injudicious firearms use," Mac said. "Our understanding is that the incident in question involved his mother's boyfriend's gun and that the weapon was a .22. Is that true?"

"Correct on both counts."

"What kind of gun was the murder weapon?"

Oscar had the satisfied look of a man who can answer a question. "The cartridge was a .380—Gibbons found the shell casing. Ballistics says six grooves with a right-hand twist. That could mean any one of a number of weapons, but I'm guessing Walther PPK\S because it's popular."

Mac raised an eyebrow.

"So what?" Oscar said. "It's not like he was going to take the boyfriend's gun again. If he listened to me, the boyfriend went out and got himself a gun safe."

"A Walther PPK\S is not exactly a Saturday night special," Mac said. "Where do you suppose Justin obtained it?"

"We'll find that out when we catch Justin. And we *will* catch Justin. Any other ideas, Mac?"

"I am interested in the contents of the victim's pockets."

"Got 'em right here." Oscar pulled out a large manila envelope from a drawer and dumped the contents on the top of his desk. A gun landed with a thud.

"He was carrying?" I said in surprise.

"Yeah, it's a standard U.S. Army weapon—Beretta M9, a 9mm Parabellum. He had a concealed carry permit for Kentucky, which is recognized in Ohio."

"Well, that's good," I said. "Otherwise you'd have to arrest his corpse. He was a security consultant, you know, so I guess a gun makes sense."

Oscar chuckled. "Security consultant? That's a pretty fancy label." He picked up the dead man's wallet and opened it to show an official card. "This license he was carrying says private investigator. It was issued by the Board of Licensure for Private Investigators in the Commonwealth of Kentucky."

Mac stroked his face where his beard used to be. "This opens up new possibilities, Oscar. Surely you see that a private detective in the course of his professional duties might acquire many enemies with motives to kill him?"

"Might? Oh, sure. It might snow tomorrow, too. I guess it's something you could work on. Maybe his sister would know something about his business."

"Was she the next of kin?"

"We don't know that yet, but her name was in his wallet. We're trying to track her down. Somebody has to claim the body."

Mac reached over and poked through the other contents of the envelope. He pushed to one side a set of keys, a smart phone, a Swiss Army knife, and a watch. The remaining stack included a couple of credit card receipts and a small paper bag containing a box about the size of a deck of cards. He looked through the receipts first.

"Here's his lunch with Polly at Daniel's. He also had dinner at Bobbie McGee's." No surprises there, but now I could erase the question mark next to McGee's on the tentative timetable of Kirtland's last day. Mac picked up the box. "What's this?"

"That was in his jacket pocket," Oscar said.

Mac opened the box. Inside lay a pair of earrings on a bed of cotton. They were jade, each about the size and shape of a dime with a rose design engraved. According to the receipt in the bag they had cost fifty dollars at Auld Lang Syne Antiques & Collectibles. There was something about the rose shape that tugged at my memory. Where had I seen . . .

"We now know another place that Kirtland visited— Auld Lang Syne," Mac said unnecessarily. "That's one more element for our timetable."

Looking at the contents of the manila envelope spread out on Oscar's desk, a thought struck me. "If he bought anything else yesterday, it's not here. He must have dropped it off at Shamrocks & Ivy. We know he went there before dinner and the play. Where were the earrings?"

"In his jacket pocket," Oscar said.

"He must have slipped them inside and either forgot or simply did not bother to remove them when he stopped at the B&B," Mac said.

"Unless he planned to give them to somebody later that night," I said. "Maybe they were a present." *Hey, that's not a bad idea!*

"I suspect that it was," Mac said, "unless he wore earrings. But for whom were they intended?"

"How should I know?" I said. "I'm making this up as I go along."

"And what difference does it make?" Oscar asked. "Whatever you're trying to get at, I'm not seeing it."

"We are simply gathering data," Mac said, "trying to find out as much as we can about Bill Kirtland's last day on this earth in the hopes that it will shed some light on *why* it was his last day and who made it that way. Jefferson mentioned that Kirtland must have put any other purchases in his room at Shamrocks & Ivy. Do you have his personal effects from that room?"

"Heh-heh." Oscar gave a low, humorless chuckle. "That's one of those things *CSI* and all of you mystery writers always get wrong. I couldn't get that stuff without a search warrant. If I expected to find something important there, I'd get one—but I don't. Once we get a hold of the victim's sister, I'm sure she'll come and claim the body, probably today. As the next of kin—presuming she is—she can go in the room and take possession of his property. That should be soon enough to find out what's there."

Mac's questions petered out at that point and I realized I had a contribution to make.

"After a pleasant chat with my future mother-in-law, I spoke to Johanna Rawls." I gave them the rundown of her acquaintance with Justin from high school, her take on what sort of dude he was, and my suggestion to her that she try to contact him through friends and get him to surrender.

"Good move, Jeff," Oscar said. "It's better for everybody all around if we get him in here the easy way. He's got a gun and somebody could get hurt, probably him."

"You have acted well, Jefferson," Mac concurred.

On that high note of approbation, we left Oscar's office and headed back to campus.

"So let me be sure I get this straight," I said. "I'm supposed to go everywhere we knew Kirtland went yesterday, plus the places we think he might have gone because Polly suggested it."

Mac nodded. "Also, in any location where they remember Kirtland, ask if he mentioned where else he was planning to go. See if anyone remembers what time they saw him. We want to build up the timetable as precisely as possible."

"Check. And what else should I ask?"

"What did he say to the clerks? Anything, no matter how seemingly inconsequential, may have some significance. Did he have anyone with him? I am sure you will think of other questions. Please give me frequent reports. Text messages would be a suitable vehicle. Do you have any other questions for me?"

I thought a moment. "Yeah. Why do you always wear bow ties?"

Both McCabe eyebrows shot up, signifying extreme surprise.

"Even in college you used to wear bow ties when everybody else wore T-shirts," I explained. "I've always wondered why, but I've never gotten around to asking you."

"Because women love them, old boy! At least, Kate does."

Chapter Sixteen
Auld Lang Syne

Incoming! I had just left Mac at his office when a text arrived.

LYNDA: *Let's elope.*

JEFF: *Too late. RSVP's are in. Can't wait to meet rest of your relatives.*

LYNDA: *SHE wants to dump DJ, get band.*

JEFF: *I'd miss Sinatra.*

LYNDA: *She's thinking Harry Connick Jr.*

JEFF: *Close enough!*

LYNDA: *Not funny. Do something!*

JEFF: *I'll talk to her later. Now gotta save Justin!*

LYNDA: *You'd better.*

I'd seen Lynda grab a weapon away from an angry murderer, but she couldn't fend off her mother's attempts to turn our simple wedding into a Hollywood production. I was supposed to do that and at the same time help Mac prove that Justin Bird didn't kill Bill Kirtland, which he probably did. I had no real idea how I was going to accomplish either. *But, hey, no pressure!*

Couldn't we just skip to the honeymoon? With that on my mind and the iPhone in my hand, I was strongly tempted to take a few minutes to check out some temperatures—from Roma to Florence. But I'm made of sterner stuff. I resolutely rejected that siren song playing in my head. Instead I did a Google Images search of the name William Kirtland. I was shocked at how many of them there are, a few of whose photos were apparently made by Matthew Brady or one of his contemporaries. It took a while but I finally found the one I knew. Now I had a picture I could show around town when I asked about him. But first, I had to tend to my day job.

I called Popcorn.

"What am I missing?"

"Ralph was sniffing around. I told him you were at lunch."

"Well, that's not a lie, just a little premature. After I go over to Caleb Wilson's antique store, I'm going to grab something to eat at Daniel's." I filled her on my mission to retrace of the murder victim's footsteps. "What did Ralph want, by the way?"

Ralph Pendergast's duties as provost and academic vice president hardly ever bring him into my orbit unless he's unhappy about something.

"He wants to know what you're going to do about all that negative coverage of Wendy Nichols shoplifting at Victoria's Secret."

"Oh, for the love of . . . You know how that works. No matter what Wendy and the Lady Dragons do this season, the sports reporters will mention the arrest in their coverage. It's like the Tiger Woods saga. If he has a bad day, it's his worst performance since he was brought down by a sex scandal. If he leads the field, it's a stunning comeback from being brought down by a sex scandal. So there's nothing I can do about media coverage of Wendy Nichols.

"Tell you what, if Ralph stops back, tell him I personally guarantee that the next time Wendy shoplifts she'll pick on a less embarrassing store. Do you think Home Depot will satisfy him?"

She didn't. I could tell by the way she chuckled.

This was no crisis. I figured it must have been a slow day and Ralph was just complaining about the media to stay in practice. He likes to pretend I can control the press, which wasn't true even when Lynda was news editor of *The Erin Observer & News-Ledger.*

"So tell me more about Lucia Schiaparelli," Popcorn pleaded.

Fifteen minutes later, after a blow-by-blow account of what happened at the *Observer* offices—and it almost *was* blow-by-blow—Popcorn finally let me go. But first I had to promise to peek down Lucia's blouse so I could report back on the designer label lurking there. The things I do to keep my staff happy.

By the time I disconnected the call, I was on Court Street, standing at the threshold of Auld Lang Syne and trying to remember whether I'd ever been there before. Antique stores tend to look alike. They have a lot of old stuff inside. This one was distinguished from the outside by a politically incorrect cigar store Indian standing in front of the building. I wished him a good day as I walked passed him, but he kept his counsel.

It was a narrow, deep building, well lit with only a faintly musty smell. I've never been sure of the dividing line between an antique store and junk shop, but this place didn't look junky. A number of glass display cases containing small items (watches, knives, fountain pens, military patches, political campaign buttons, and so forth) stood near the front door. On the walls, against the walls, on the floor, and in wood cases around the store were all manner of old clocks, hats, shot glasses, ice buckets, cocktail shakers (I liked the one shaped like a penguin), dresses, jewelry, bar signs, mirrors, tables, chairs, radios (Crosley was big), record albums, books, magazines with pictures of Jackie Kennedy, crafts, dolls, photographs, commemorative bourbon bottles, little red wagons, nutcrackers, rugs, Santa Clauses, sleds, guns, tools, Coca-Cola coolers, playing cards, lunch boxes, cigar boxes, and store clerks.

Music was playing in the background, a succession of soft-rock classics like "Save the Last Dance for Me," "Dream Lover," "I Only Have Eyes for You, and "Bye-Bye Love" to set a nostalgic (and buying) mood.

Right away I spotted Caleb Wilson behind one of the display cases, and he saw me about the same time. He looked different without the false mustache he sported on stage while playing Dr. Watson, though not as much different as Mac did without his beard. He had a high forehead that made him look much older than me, although he wasn't. His hair, what there was of it, was closely cropped but not shaved. In a checked shirt and chinos, he wasn't dressed for the stage.

"How are you today, sir?" he asked with a big smile, apparently not recognizing me.

Oh, same old, same old—just another fun day of trying to make the woman I love happy by proving the most likely murder suspect is innocent and getting her fabulously beautiful and famous mother to dial down her wedding fascism.

"Better than I deserve," I said truthfully. I looked around. "You have a nice store. It reminds me of the place I'm staying."

"Where's that?"

"Shamrocks & Ivy, over on College Street."

"Oh, sure. George and Sally have been shopping here ever since they bought the place. They always want to negotiate down the price." He squinted, as if to see me better. "Say, don't you live here in town? You're Professor McCabe's brother-in-law, aren't you?"

"No, I'm Kate McCabe's brother."

His brain seemed to have a tough time processing that, so I let him off the hook by conceding that he had me pegged. I briefly explained that I had temporarily moved out of my apartment so that my future father-in-law could move in. I didn't mention that the man who had taken over my happy home was a jealous, gun-toting, retired Army officer who had an obsession for his ex-wife currently domiciled just a few yards away on the same property. Why worry him? Since Mac was the link between us, and he knew Mac from the Lyceum Players, I asked him how the play was going.

"Wow! How do I answer that?" *Actually, that was just a piece of content-free conversation filler. You can move on if you want to.* He didn't want to. "I haven't talked to any other cast members, but I assume they're all as shook up as I am. We had a great night, our first show and the audience loved us, and then *bam!*—a murder right in our own back yard, so to speak!"

When somebody opens the door for you, dive in.

"The murder is just what I wanted to talk to you about."

He frowned. "What do you mean, talk to me? I don't know anything about it except what I read in the paper."

"You might know something important about the victim, though. Let me explain." So I gave him the *Cliffs Notes* version of my mission on behalf of Sebastian McCabe.

"So you're like his Watson!" Wilson said at the end.

"I really try to avoid that comparison. I mean, who wants to be Watson?"

"I do." He spread his arms. "It's a great role. He's a lover, a fighter, and a good right hand. Whenever Holmes needs him, which is a lot, he's there at his side—a man of action. In this play he even breaks the law because Holmes asks him to. Watson is plenty smart, but no genius. Neither am I. So I can imagine being Watson, but I can't imagine being Sherlock Holmes. By the way—and don't tell Jonny Hawes this— Holmes needs Watson more than Watson needs Holmes."

Sorry I asked.

But that actually made sense, kind of. I'd have to remember that while I was trudging around town showing Bill Kirtland's photo and Mac was sitting on his rump back at his office. I pulled out the iPhone and showed Wilson the picture I'd turned up from Google Images.

"This is the murdered man. Does he look familiar?"

"I don't think so."

"He was in your store yesterday. We know that because he bought some earrings." That sounded accusatory, even to me, so I added: "You may not have been here when he was, or maybe you just didn't notice him."

"It's a big store and I don't see everybody who comes in. We do a fair trade with parents who are in town to check out St. Benignus for their kids. Let's ask Maisie. She sells a lot of jewelry."

Within a minute he was introducing me to Mrs. Weisgerber. She was a bird-like woman in a black dress and blue stockings, with big rings on both hands and a silver chain around her heavily wrinkled neck. Also around her neck was another chain with a pair of glasses whose frames matched the red of her lipstick. Her ears were doubly pierced and hung with ornaments like a Christmas tree. I figured she could have started collecting her full Social Security payments something like twenty years ago if she'd wanted, never mind the dyed black hair. She stood next to a glass cabinet hosting numerous pins, earrings, bracelets, necklaces, and other jewelry.

After Wilson gave her the rundown of what I was up to, I showed her Kirtland's picture.

When she spoke she had the raspy voice of a heavy cigarette smoker. I bet she liked martinis, too.

"Sure I remember him," she said. "Good looking fella. He bought a nice little pair of rose earrings. I remember the earrings because they were jade, but the design was rose. Who ever heard of a green rose?" Her eyes were black and alert. "It was unusual, you know?"

"That's the guy I'm asking about, all right," I said. "Do you remember what time that was?"

"It was after lunch, and I eat late. Maybe two or three o'clock, somewhere in there."

"Was he by himself?"

"Yeah."

"What did he say?"

"Not much. I asked him if I could help him find anything and he said he was just looking. But he ended up buying."

I was looking myself. One of the enamel pins in the case was in the shape of a parrot, lots of bright colors. Lynda likes pins, and she would think this one was cute. It would look great with one of her red dresses. But there was another one lying near it, a gold and green cat with emerald eyes, that was also nice and didn't cost as much. I looked from one to the other, trying to decide.

"May I give you some advice, young man?" Maisie rasped.

"What's that?"

"Don't settle."

I didn't get it. "What do you mean?"

"If you want something, don't settle for anything less. It's not worth it. You'll regret it later. That's what I told that fella who bought the rose earrings. He was trying to decide between those and this pair"—she pointed to a set of porcelain rose earrings priced at twenty dollars—"and I told him not to settle."

My heart was racing. "He must have said *something* at that point."

She nodded. "Yeah, I remember now that he did. He held up the jade pair and he said, 'These will be perfect for a very special person.'"

Chapter Seventeen
Never Too Late

I chewed on that, along with my peanut butter and banana sandwich—"The Elvis"—at Daniel's Apothecary a few minutes after leaving Auld Lang Syne with Lynda's pin in my pocket.

Daniel's is the iconic Erin establishment, the one that everybody told me about when I'd first arrived in town as a college student twenty years earlier. It's one of those places where town and gown meet—the kids think the soda shop décor is delightfully retro and the townies have grown up with the place. It's been owned by the Daniel family since 1904. I don't know if the jukebox and the posters of Marilyn Monroe and James Dean arrived in the 1950s and just stayed there or were added during some nostalgia craze. Either way, it's kind of cool and certainly a break from the chain restaurants.

So I sat there eating my sandwich, nursing a caffeine-free Diet Coke, and tried to build a scenario around the earrings. *I should be able to do that. I'm a writer, right?*

Okay, try this: The "special person" for whom Bill Kirtland was buying the earrings had a jealous husband or boyfriend who took Kirtland's attentions amiss. That wasn't too far-fetched, except who was the special person? Triple M? No, that was no good—that would point to Justin as the jealous killer! This wasn't going well. Wait a minute. Triple M doesn't wear earrings. I've known sisters who do, but not her. So that lets her out! That was a relief. But wait a minute, maybe she used to wear earrings and Kirtland didn't realize that she'd stopped. Were her ears pierced? I'd never noticed.

This wasn't helping. Triple M, Sister Mary Margaret Malone, so far as we could tell was the only person Kirtland knew in Erin before coming here. Did the jealous boyfriend/husband scenario still have legs if the intended recipient of the earrings didn't live here? Yeah, I decided, it could work if the killer came to Erin just to do away with Kirtland. But why would he do that? To distance himself from the scene of the crime! Because Kirtland was killed in Erin, the police were looking in Erin for the killer—not in Louisville or wherever the killer lived.

Hey, that worked! But why stop there? What other possibilities were there involving the earrings?

As the waitress refilled my glass of Diet Coke, I keep repeating the word *earrings* to myself, trying to remember another context in which I'd heard that word recently. It nagged at me . . . until I had it! Amy Quong had complained of missing earrings. She didn't say they were jade, but isn't jade associated with China? And wasn't Amy Quong Chinese? Okay, suppose the earrings that Kirtland bought at Auld Lang Syne were hers, meaning they'd been stolen and Kirtland knew it. He bought them to get the evidence that Auld Lang Syne was dealing in stolen goods.

My excitement lasted about ten seconds until I realized that scenario had more holes than a garden soaker. Who would kill somebody to hide a fifty dollar theft? Why kill him hours after the purchase, by which time he could have already told Amy Quong and the police what he'd learned? And how would the killer—Caleb Wilson?—even know that Kirtland was on to him? But Wilson couldn't be the killer anyway because he was in the play; he would have had to bring someone else in on it.

I was starting to get a headache.

Well, I thought gloomily, at least the first scenario still worked. But the jealous husband or boyfriend was only a theory. What had I learned for sure from my interview with Maisie Weisgerber? I thought about that for a few moments and then sent Mac a text by way of report:

K visited ALS alone at 2 or 3 pm. Bought earrings for unnamed "very special person." Not likely Polly. Girlfriend? Husband or boyfriend jealous? Now at Daniel's.

As I was admiring the pithy accuracy of my writing, I heard somebody call my name.

"Jeff? Jeff Cody, is that you?" The Colonel, my future father-in-law was heading toward my table. "What a coincidence. This really is a small town, isn't it?" *Well, 29,098 is no metropolis. But this week it feels like Erin has two people too many.* "Mind if I join you?"

He was already pulling up a chair, making both his question and my answer superfluous.

"Not at all, Colonel. Good to see you." *Just don't pull out your gun. Jacqui Daniel would faint dead away.*

Still getting used to the idea that Lynda's father was a real person, not just a military title, I gave him the once over not so lightly. The loose-fitting short-sleeve shirt he was wearing, not tucked it, made it impossible for me to tell whether he was packing right now or not. But it hardly mattered. His forearms could have been registered as lethal weapons. He must have been working out since before I was born. The gray of his hair did nothing to detract either from his impression of strength or from his good looks. He and Lucia were maybe the handsomest couple I'd ever known, as well as the oddest.

"I looked in here through the window and I just couldn't stop myself from coming in," he said. "This reminds me of when I was a kid in Decatur, Georgia, in the 1950s, except that Pepsi signs weren't allowed—that was Coca-Cola country. The corner drug store had a soda fountain just like that." He nodded in the direction of the long counter and stools serving up fountain sodas and milkshakes made with

Hershey's ice cream. "That was a good time to grow up, the 1950s."

Thanks for this trip down memory lane, Colonel, but I—

"Hi, Jeff."

"Oh, hello there, Trixie." Damn. I should have kept it business-like, called her Dr. LaBelle. *I hardly know that woman, Colonel, and I've certainly never noticed that she's pretty and vivacious.*

The Colonel gave my urologist a hairy eyeball as she walked past us on her way out. Fortunately her lush auburn hair was pinned up and she was wearing a no-nonsense pair of black slacks that gave no hint of the nice legs beneath. "Friend of yours?" the Colonel asked casually as he picked up a menu. He regarded me with steel in his gray eyes.

"Actually she's my, uh, doctor."

"Get sick a lot, do you?"

You mean, how often do I visit this woman? "Hardly ever at all, sir. I'm in excellent health. I work out. But, you know, we all get sick sometimes." *It sure is warm in here.*

Incoming! Upon hearing that muted buzz, I pulled my smart phone out of my pocket and looked at it discretely under the table. It was a text from Mac: *Well done. Carry on.* I felt like a dog who'd just been patted on the head by his master, except a dog would be more pleased.

"What's good to eat here?" my father-in-law-to-be inquired, holding up the menu. I noticed that the waitress, Vern, was about three feet away and had her pad out.

Col. Jacob Teal struck me as the sort of man who wanted a quick and firm answer, so I gave him one. Figuring him for a red meat eater, I said, "You'd probably like the Big Bopper Burger"—*a.k.a., Heart Attack on a Plate*—"it's a half pound of beef with tomatoes and onion, fries on the side." *Or you could just have the cholesterol injected intravenously.*

"That's what I'll have, then," the Colonel told Vern. "I had my eye on the peanut butter and banana, but he talked me out of it. And I want a chocolate milkshake with extra chocolate. If you're going to be a kid, you might as well go all the way. I don't indulge often."

That I can believe.

When Vern had left, amid cheerful assurances that the order would be "coming right up," the Colonel put away the menu and gave me his full attention.

"So," he said, "you're going to marry my Lynda. I don't recall you asking my permission, son."

My heart started palpitating and I felt faint. Then I noticed that the Colonel's mouth was twisted. For a horrifying moment I thought that he'd had a stroke. Then I realized he was smiling. That was his idea of a joke! What was next for laughs, waterboarding?

"Is it too late?" I asked.

"It's never too late, son. Say, how about if I call you Jeff and you call me Jake?"

"I'd like it better if you call me Jeff and I call you Colonel."

He nodded slowly. "That works, too. I read your books, you know. Good stuff. Your description of Lynda was right on target. And I love the way you exaggerated your neurotic tendencies for comic effect. I got quite a chuckle out of that."

Actually, I wasn't exaggerating. "Gee, thanks. How do you like my apartment?"

He gave a long answer in which he tactfully said "cozy" several times instead of "cramped." We talked meaninglessly like that for a few minutes while I worked out what I really wanted to say and how I was going to say it. Just when I had it nailed, Vern brought the Colonel's burger. When he bit into it, and his mouth was full, I unloaded.

"Maybe what I'm going to say should be obvious, Colonel, but we live in a strange world, so I'm going to say it anyway just for the record. The thing is, I'm in love with your daughter and I have been for years. I know that's not all it takes to make a marriage, but I think the two of us have what it does take. We've been through a lot together—you've read about some of it—and we're prepared to go through more. We're totally committed to each other, and for the long haul."

Nervous now, and afraid the Colonel would stick in his two cents' worth if I lost momentum, I began talking faster.

"Obviously, I want the best for her and I want her to be happy in every way—especially on the day we marry. Lynda planned this wedding the way she wanted it, low-key and spiritual and no bridesmaids dressed like Lady Gaga. Now her mother's making her miserable by trying to kidnap the whole wedding with a bunch of over-the-top add-ons. What I'm wondering is if you can help me find the off-switch on that."

As many times as I've read the word "guffaw," I'd never actually heard one until then. The Colonel guffawed, causing him to almost choke on his Big Bopper Burger. He set the sandwich down.

"Jeff, if I could find that switch, Lucia and I would still be married. I don't know what Lynda told you"—*almost nothing!*—"but the divorce wasn't my idea. I never remarried and I'd take her back right now, in spite of everything. I love that woman."

That wasn't at all what I'd expected to hear from Colonel Cool. He sighed. "Being in the Army, traveling around the world for most of my career, I never had the chance to be the kind of father I wanted to be for my girls. I just hope that what I said before is true."

He lost me there. "What's that?"

"That it's never too late." He took a long, bracing sip of his milkshake. "Frankly, Lucia was never Mother of the Year, but her mother was a saint, God rest her soul. The girls turned out well. I'm really proud of them. You'll take care of Lynda, won't you?"

"We'll take care of each other, Colonel."

He nodded and finished his sandwich in silence, either because he didn't want to say any more or because he couldn't. I sipped my Diet Coke, wondering whether he was normally this self-revealing with near strangers, or only with future sons-in-law, or whether the emotions of the coming nuptials had him in their grip.

"So," he said, shoving away his empty plate, "tell me about yourself, Jeff."

I looked at my watch. "I'd love to." *It's a fascinating subject.* "But I've really got to get back to work."

"Public relations work or detective work?"

That was a question I sure hadn't seen coming. "Detective work? What do you mean?"

"I had breakfast with Lynda this morning. All she wanted to talk about was you." While I was busy grinning like an idiot, he added: "She told me all about how you and Mac are trying to clear the suspect in that murder last night. Based on your track record, I'd say that if Sister Polly's friend is innocent he couldn't have anybody better than you and your brother-in-law in his corner."

I stood up. "Thank you, Colonel. I'll certainly try to justify your confidence."

"Maybe I can help." He got up as well.

Not sure at first how to answer that, I settled on the factual approach. "I'm trying to retrace Bill Kirtland's steps yesterday, build a timetable, and talk to anybody he had contact with. Maybe he was with somebody else or said something that might prove helpful."

"That sounds like a long shot."

I nodded. "It is. But sometimes long shots pay off. So I'm going to an antique store, a bookstore, and a winery—all places we have reason to believe he went. And if I get a line on someplace else he might have gone, I'll go there, too."

"Can I tag along?"

"What for? No offense."

"None taken. We can talk while we walk, get to know each other a little."

I wouldn't mind that. And I'd never been all that crazy about doing this by myself anyway. "Okay, you're on. Let's go."

Chapter Eighteen
Collectibles

We started out right next door at Garrison's Antiques and Collectibles. The small store was jammed with goods, making for a cramped feel.

"Looks like my grandmother's attic in Decatur," Col. Teal murmured.

My mother complains of feeling old when she goes into an antique store and finds the toys and games of her own childhood on display. I knew how she felt as I looked around at the Cabbage Patch dolls, Beanie Babies, Coleco Adam computers, and *Star Wars* toys. *Those must be the collectibles, not the antiques.*

"Good afternoon, gentleman, may I help you?"

The Colonel and I spun around to face the inquirer. Leonidis Garrison, with whom I've had a nodding acquaintance over the years, is a stout fellow with a walrus mustache, longish hair, and wire-rimmed glasses. He stands about half a foot shorter than me so that I had to peer down to admire his Three Stooges tie.

I gave him the thirty-second synopsis of what we were about and showed him Bill Kirtland's picture on my smart phone.

"Yeah, I remember him. He said he was just looking."

Garrison was wearing suspenders over his short-sleeved white shirt as well as a belt, which I take to be the mark of a man who takes no chances. I figured that he probably kept a close eye on customers wandering around his store.

"Was he looking at anything in particular?" I asked.

"He spent a lot of time looking at the *Millennium Falcon*. He said Han Solo was his favorite *Star Wars* character." *Isn't he everybody's?*

"Was he alone?" Col. Teal asked.

"Yep."

"He didn't buy anything?" the Colonel pressed.

"Nope."

A few more questions established that he also didn't say much. Neither did Garrison. I thanked the store owner for his time and we left.

"On to Pages Gone By," I said.

"Not so fast." Col. Teal held up a small pamphlet, an 8½ by 14 sheet of paper folded in thirds. At the top it said "Visit Erin's Antiques & Specialty Shops." Below was a list of a dozen stores and a small map of some of the major downtown streets. "If Kirtland shopped at two antique stores, he probably hit others as well."

"Where'd you get that?" I asked.

"It was on a table where we walked in."

"You don't miss much, do you?"

"Not if I can help it."

We decided to stop in at as many of the stores as we could on the way to Pages Gone By, then double back and visit some others if we had any time after driving out to Silk Stocking Winery. As we walked, I gave him the essential Thomas Jefferson Cody biography: born in Virginia thirty-seven years ago, went to college at St. Benignus after the University of Virginia didn't work out, got a work-study job in the college public relations department, planned to get a masters degree in journalism somewhere else but never got around to it, stayed on at St. Benignus instead.

"How did you meet Lynda?"

"On the job. She was a reporter at *The Erin Observer & News-Ledger* then. That must have been close to six years ago, so Lynda was in her early twenties and a few years out of school.

The college was one of her beats and she used to take me out to lunch a lot. I really liked that, and her, so I got very aggressive about calling her with story ideas. Eventually I asked her out. We've been dating for five years now. About a year ago we had what turned out to be a trial separation for about a month and it failed miserably." *The hiatus was four weeks and two days, to be precise, and it wasn't my idea.* "We're meant to be together, Colonel."

If he wanted any more intimate details about the Teal-Cody relationship, he wasn't going to get them. But he didn't ask.

"I envy you," was all he said.

Touched by his simple sincerity, I let that lie there for now. But I was pretty sure I'd pick it up some other time.

We showed Bill Kirtland's picture and asked our questions at Memories, Things Past, Sgt. Pepper's Vintage Clothes, Act II, and The Treasure Chest. The last was located right next to Pages Gone By on High Street. That was a good thing, because my feet were sore and all the stores were running together in my mind. Sure, they each had their own niche, but they all had their similarities, too.

"Well, that was a lot of nothing," I told the Colonel as we left the Treasure Chest, about to enter the used book store.

"I wonder what McCabe would make of it."

"Oh, him. I guess I should check in."

I pulled out my smart phone and sent Mac a text summarizing a couple of hours of gumshoe legwork:

Confirmed Kirtland sighting at Memories and Act II. Bought nothing. Haven't found your wild goose yet, but still chasing.

Understandably, the clerks at those stores didn't remember what time Kirtland had been there. But the one at Act II remembered that he'd been carrying a small package, so that may have been after his purchase at Auld Lang Syne.

Without waiting for a text response from Mac, we went into Pages Gone By. The store was somehow big and cozy at the same time, with lots of space carved up into little rooms so that you could exercise your passion for mysteries in one alcove while your mate was off in Fantasyland in another. But there was a front desk with a clerk, and I knew her.

"Hi, Mo," I said.

"Hello yourself, big boy."

Col. Teal regarded me with raised eyebrows. *What, I can't have friends?*

Maureen Russert is a pleasant-looking divorcee a couple of years older than I am, close to forty. I used to tease her about being a cougar when I took her out. She was the only woman I'd dated since meeting Lynda. It had happened during that four-week period when Lynda was on sabbatical from me. A three-toed sloth could count on one hand the number times. We'd had lots of laughs, but no sparks on either side. Our friendship survived the experience. I'd never felt awkward around her until now, with my future father-in-law at my side. Lynda and I had invited her to the wedding.

With her freckles and her straight, dark hair in bangs at the front and long at the back, she looked younger than her years. I could never figure out why that stuffy Arthur Bancroft Russert had traded her in for a younger model. But then, there are a lot of things in this world that I don't understand—such as why the mystery section in Pages Gone By is marked off with a silhouette of Sherlock Holmes. Why not Mike Hammer?

"You look like a man on a mission," Mo said.

"I could never hide anything from you. Not that I wanted to." *Wait, that didn't sound right.* "What I mean is, we *are* on a mission. This is Lynda's dad, Col. Jacob Teal."

"Jake," he said, putting out his hand.

Mo took it. "Pleased to meet you. What's up?"

I showed her the Google Images photo on my smart phone. "We're wondering whether this man came into the store yesterday."

"Oh, that's the poor man who was shot last night! I saw his picture on *The Observer*'s website." It hadn't made the print edition. "Yeah, he was in here yesterday."

Bingo!

"What time was that?"

"I was just coming back from lunch, so almost two o'clock, maybe one forty-five, but don't tell my boss because I was running late."

"Did he buy anything?"

"Yeah, a mystery novel."

The genre was Mo's special passion, as it was mine. Her dream of opening her own mystery book store was every bit as strong as mine of writing private eye novels had once been. My bet was on her.

Incoming! "Excuse me, Mo." I thought maybe Mac was responding to my report with a hearty *Good work, old boy!* or perhaps a word of encouragement to hang in there. But it was my beloved who was texting me.

LYNDA: *L is reading wedding porn!!!!!*

JEFF: *???????*

LYNDA: *Brides magazines. In my office! Need cigarette.*

JEFF: *NO!!! You quit.*

LYNDA: *She won't leave.*

JEFF: *Call cops. Am at Pages with your father.*

LYNDA: *W/ daddy? WTH? Tell Mo hi.*

I got a creepy feeling at the back of my neck at the last three words. I'd never told Lynda about taking Mo to that vampire movie. It didn't seem important. But it wasn't as if I'd lied—I mean, I didn't *deny* going out with her; the subject just never came up. *I wonder if Mo*—I put the smart phone back in my pocket and tried to shove the subject to the far reaches of my mind.

"Sorry. You were saying he bought a mystery."

"Yeah. I remember it was an old paperback edition of *Hocus-Pocus* by Sebastian McCabe. That's the one where Damon

Devlin's magician friend disappears on stage from a box and never re-appears. It turns out he's been kidnapped. Mr. Kirtland said he wanted to read it again."

Well, that was another reason Mac should be asking all these questions instead of me.

"Do you have any more McCabe books?" Col. Teal asked.

"Sure. They're popular around here, this being where he lives and all. They're right over there in the mystery nook. Rows and rows of them."

Just rub it in, Mo.

"I'd like to pick up a few," the Colonel said. "I've never read his stuff."

I cut into this McCabe love fest to get back to the business at hand. "Can you remember anything else Kirtland said?" I asked Mo.

She bit a lip. "Just small talk, I think. He said he was just passing through town and stopped to see a friend. Oh, then he made a joke out of it. He lowered his voice and said he was a private eye on a case."

"That's interesting," I said.

"Why?" Mo put her hand on her hip and a quizzical expression on her face. Had she slimmed down some over the last year or was it just the cut of her jeans?

"Because he really was a private detective. So if he told you the truth about that, maybe he really was on a case."

She smiled brightly. "You mean I helped."

"Too soon to tell, but I'll let you know. Thanks, Mo."

"Sure. Hey, I'm looking forward to the wedding. Lynda is a lucky girl."

I gave her my best *aw, shucks* smile, but before I could respond with the conventional (but true) "Lynda's the lucky one," the Colonel intervened with his own verdict: "I think he'll do."

That was my biggest surprise of the day.

Chaapter Nineteen
Wine and Weapons

Just outside the store, I texted Mac: *K told Mo he was PI on a case. Joking?* I sent that, thought a moment, and then added: *Another fact: K had horrible taste in lit.* Let him puzzle over that one.

"Polly recommended the Farmer's Market to Kirtland, but it's only open on Tuesdays, Thursdays, and Saturdays, so I guess we should go out to the winery," I told Col. Teal. "You want to drive?" If he was so hell-bent on playing amateur sleuth, let him burn up the gas at almost four bucks a gallon.

"Sure. I'm parked in *The Observer's* lot. I figured if I got towed Lynda could get me off the hook."

My smart phone vibrated and I snuck a look at the message. This time it was Mac. *Most satisfactory!*

Since I usually pedal my Schwinn everywhere I go, my Volkswagen New Beetle is my idea of a luxury conveyance. The Colonel's new Buick Lucerne was like being a first-class passenger on a top airline—in my imagination, anyway.

I leaned back against the leather. Col. Teal put half a dozen just-purchased Sebastian McCabe paperbacks on the floor behind his seat.

"You must be quite the ladies man," the Colonel said conversationally as he got behind the wheel. "Everywhere you go you seem to have female friends."

Just when I thought he was starting to like me.

"Oh, well, you know. I have friends. Some are guys, some are gals. I mean everybody has to be one or the other, right? Except hermaphrodites, they're both. But I don't know any of them." *I hate it when I babble. It's hot for May, isn't it? I wish my phone would ring.*

My phone rang. I grabbed it out of my front pocket like a gunslinger pulling his six-shooter out of his holster. (Somehow Col. Teal inspired gun metaphors.) I didn't recognize the phone number so I answered with, "Jeff Cody here."

"I didn't do it Mr. Cody!" The words came out in a rush.

Involuntarily, my hand tightened its grip on the smart phone. "Justin? Is this Justin?"

"Yeah. It's Justin. I didn't kill that man."

I wondered for maybe three seconds how he had my cell number, but that was no mystery. Approximately four thousand people have my cell number and he could have gotten it from any one of them—Triple M, Johanna, or maybe a friend of a friend.

"We're trying to help you, Justin, but you have to help yourself," I said. "Turn yourself in. You don't have to go the chief by yourself. I'm sure Sister Polly would go with you." I thought that would make it easier for him, but I was wrong.

"I can't do that!" Justin said. "I let her down. I don't want her to be disappointed in me."

I looked at Col. Teal. He could hear Justin and was listening intently.

"What do you mean, you let her down?" I asked.

"The reason I saw that body, Mr. Cody, I was going out to catch a smoke. Sister Polly thinks I quit."

The kid was wanted for murder and he was afraid Triple M was going to find out he had succumbed to his nicotine addiction. The trouble with fiction is, you can't make stuff like that up. Who would believe it? It was hard work keeping my cool, not screaming at the idiot.

"Uh, Justin, I'm sure Sister Polly will get over the disappointment. You have a much bigger problem than that.

The longer you stay in hiding, the guiltier you look. You have to turn yourself in. I'll take you in if you want."

"I didn't kill nobody," he said, and hung up.

I cursed at the phone. Col. Teal glanced briefly my way. "Lynda's going to have an interesting life being married to you, isn't she?"

"I'm afraid so, Colonel."

"You know, I didn't catch all the details of this case. Why do the cops think this Justin fellow did it?"

I ran down the basic facts—Justin's history of shooting up the bus and how he had called 911 about Kirtland's murder, but left the scene after Oscar specifically told him not to. Col. Teal asked about the gun used in the shooting.

"Oscar said it was a Walther PPK/S .380."

The Colonel nodded. "A fine firearm. A lot of guys use it as a backup weapon."

"Backup?" I echoed.

"Sure. Professionals—military, police officers, people like that—usually don't carry just one gun."

"So, do you have a backup?"

"Colt .32. Want to see it?"

"That won't be necessary. Mac has one of those." I keep expecting my brother-in-law to shoot his foot off with it. "What kind of work does a retired Army colonel with two concealed weapons do?"

"I'm not doing any work yet. I'll find something that fits. I'm not in a hurry."

"What did you do in the Army?"

"I killed people." After a beat, he added with a deadpan expression, "That's my standard answer. I like to remind people that we live in a dangerous world and war isn't a video game. Of course, I didn't kill people at the Pentagon, although sometimes I wanted to. I suppose with my contacts in Washington I could work for a military contractor of some

sort, but it would have to be something interesting. I'm not
ready for a rocking chair."

When he said "defense contractor," right away I
thought of Blackwater, that private security company—kind of
a for-profit army—that got in trouble for some of the
unpleasant things its people did in Iraq while under contract to
the United States government. The company was still around,
but had changed its name a couple of times.

"The Altiora Corp. has a couple of subsidiaries in Erin
that do Defense Department work," I offered.

"Is that so?"

"Probably not in your line, though."

Just what is your line? You didn't really answer.

"Probably not. I'd like to get back overseas again." I
didn't think he meant Rome. "Of course, if I had grandchildren
in this area . . ."

I'll do my best!

"Oh, I forgot to tell you, Colonel, Lynda sent me a text
while we were in the book store. Apparently Lucia has been
camped out in Lynda's office reading brides magazines and
sharing new insights about how awful the wedding is going to
be. Do you think maybe you could talk to your ex about that
tonight, get her to ease up a little?"

He shook his head. "Won't see her. Polly invited her to
the bachelorette party tonight."

Oh no.

Triple M, as maid of honor, had performed the
traditional duty of organizing a bachelorette party. Of course, it
wouldn't be the raunchy affair those events usually deteriorated
into. She had hired the top chef at Ricoletti's Ristorante to give
a demonstration in gourmet cooking for the guests, which
would include Kate, Johanna Rawls, Popcorn, Megan Whitlock
(Lynda's boss), and a number of other friends. It was a sweet
idea that Triple M had gotten from a wedding book. Still, with
Lucia on the scene, I had visions of the evening turning into a
disaster. In retrospect, I was being optimistic.

"In fact," Col. Teal added, "I don't have any dinner plans. How about you?"

"I thought that after we're finished at the winery, I'd go to Bobbie McGee's because that's where Bill Kirtland had his last meal."

"Okay, I'm in. Lead on, Holmes."

Well, if he was going to put it like that, how could I tell him no?

Silk Stocking Winery, a ten-minute drive from downtown Erin, is part of a burgeoning regional wine industry in Ohio, Kentucky, and Indiana. There's even a Kentucky Wine Trail just like the more famous Kentucky Bourbon Trail (on which my bourbon-loving fiancée has dragged me several times, by the way).

We pulled up to a long, low building set on several acres of vines and walked inside. A young man in a pony tail stood behind a counter pouring wine into small glasses for a middle-age couple sitting on bar stools. "Now this red is going to be sweeter," he said.

Killing time, we wandered around the room looking at the racks of wine along with coasters, stoppers, bar signs, wine racks, wine-glass holders, wine bags, corkscrews, wine-themed jewelry, and other fruit-of-the-vine paraphernalia. I looked at the wine labels as if they actually meant something to me. In reality, my knowledge of wine is pretty much limited to knowing that it can be expensive, and that for Jeff Cody it never will be. I try to sound sophisticated when I order the house red.

"Nice legs," Col. Teal commented out of the side of his mouth. This observation was not directed at some comely lass but at the label plastered on Silk Stocking wines. It was a shapely leg clad in a black fishnet stocking, reminiscent of the leg lamp in *A Christmas Story*. I love black fishnet stockings. Lynda never wears them.

"Funny name for a winery," the Colonel said.

"No stranger than Blue Nun or Fat Bastard," I noted.

"Good point."

The customers left, each carrying a bottle or two in a bag, and the clerk turned his attention to us. The nametag on his white Silk Stocking polo shirt told us his name was Gene, but not whether he was a member of the Costello family that owned the winery. I suspected that he was.

"Would you gentlemen like to taste some wine today?"

Normally that question would have been either dumb or rhetorical, except that this time the answer was no. We were here on a mission, and it wasn't to sample adult beverages.

"Sure," Col. Teal said before I had the chance to reply in the negative. *You're just full of surprises, aren't you, Colonel?*

So the two of us plunked ourselves down on adjoining bar stools. Gene gave us a piece of paper listing the whole gamut of Silk Stocking wines from which we were to choose the ones we wanted to sample at fifty cents a mini-glass. With knowledgeable commentary, he led us through half a dozen wines from dry to sweet, and from white to red. By the end I was a bit light-headed and Gene was bagging up two bottles of merlot for the Colonel. Time to get to work.

I pulled out my smart phone and accessed the photo of Bill Kirtland.

"Does this guy look familiar to you?" I held up the phone for Gene to see. "We understand he bought a bottle of wine here yesterday."

"Yeah, I remember him—he was a Riesling. He did a tasting just like you guys and he bought a bottle of Riesling."

"What time was that?"

"Why do you want to know?" His tone wasn't argumentative or in-your-face, but it was cautious. Maybe he thought we were revenuers or something.

"Because he was murdered yesterday," my companion said bluntly.

"Oh, my God! That guy who was shot? That's him? People have been talking about it all day long but I never dreamed that he was a customer. Are you guys cops?"

Once upon a time, on another murder case, a witness assumed that I was a police officer and I didn't correct him. But if I answered Gene's point blank question with a lie, I would be impersonating an officer of the law. That was a bridge too far, and a bridge I would not cross, and whatever other clichés of your own that you might want to add. I was still thinking about how to answer truthfully and yet get Gene to cooperate when the Colonel spoke up.

"I am Col. Jacob A. Teal of U.S. Army Intelligence and this man is Thomas Jefferson Cody." He flashed some kind of official-looking ID card so fast a graduate of the Evelyn Wood speed-reading course would have been left behind. Was he a 97 Bravo too? "We'd really appreciate your help in this sensitive matter."

Gene swallowed. "Oh, man. You mean it's national security?"

"Well, I can't really say."

"Hey, I have a brother in the Air Force. What do you want to know?"

"What time was Bill Kirtland here?" I asked.

"It was about this time yesterday, late afternoon."

"Was he alone?"

"Yeah, but I had the feeling he wasn't going to be."

"What do you mean?"

"He said he bought the wine for a friend of his who really likes Riesling."

"Did this friend have a name?" Col. Teal pressed.

"I remember that he said right before he left, 'I'm sure Polly will love it.'"

Polly! That wasn't a shock, but it was an interesting piece of information.

"Did he say anything else while he was here?" I asked.

"Nothing special. I mean, he asked a few questions about the wine during the tasting. He seemed to like the cabernet sauvignon, but he bought the Riesling. Then he left and that other guy followed him out."

Again I had that creepy feeling at the back of my neck. "What other guy?"

"Some tall dude with a shaved head and snake tattoos on his arms—not the kind of guy I'd like to meet in a dark alley, that's for sure. He came in a minute or two after the customer and stood over there behind that rack, like he was hiding or something. After the customer left he did, too. I didn't think that much about it at the time—we get all kinds here—but I guess that could be important, huh?"

"I wouldn't doubt it," I said gloomily.

Chapter Twenty

Me and Bobbie McGee's

"Army intelligence?" I prompted.

"I had to say something to get him talking," Col. Teal said. "Apparently his B.S. meter is not very finely tuned. This ID certifies that I'm retired military so I can shop at the PX." He held out his wallet so I could see. "It's not doing me a lot of good in Erin, by the way."

We were sitting in Bobbie McGee's Sports Bar, waiting for a waitress to take our order. The place was wallpapered with televisions, about half of them tuned to Fox News and the rest to ESPN. I was multi-tasking, texting Mac while I was talking to the Colonel. A lot had happened since my last text, and it was a challenge to put it concisely. I came up with:

"*J called, denied murder.*" I'd fill Mac in later on the more horrible crime of smoking. "*K bought MMM a bottle of wine. Clerk says J followed K to winery!*" After consideration, I changed the exclamation point to a period so Mac wouldn't accuse me of sensationalizing. "*Looks bad for J.*" I erased that; why state the obvious?

I could write text messages a lot faster if I didn't think about it.

"My name is Mindy and I'll be your server this evening. Are we having something to drink first?"

I looked up. Mindy was young, pretty, and built like a brick pizza parlor. I immediately concentrated on the menu she had just handed me. My future father-in-law seemed to think I had a roving eye; I didn't want to feed his totally unfounded fantasy.

"Bourbon on the rocks," the Colonel said. So he had the same taste in adult beverages as Lynda—or, more likely, vice versa. She apparently has more refined tastes, though, because he didn't ask what brands were available the way she would have.

Bobbie McGee's is not one of my regular haunts, but I've been there often enough to know that caffeine-free Diet Coke is not among the offerings. "I'll have a Hudy Delight," I told Mindy.

"Don't let me have more than one," I told the Colonel when she'd gone. He nodded as if to say "Deal!" My first beer usually leads to a second, and the second makes me surly, which is why I usually don't have the first unless I'm feeling very much in control of myself.

"We didn't help Polly's friend very much today, did we?" Col. Teal asked.

"The term 'assisted suicide' does spring to mind."

Instead of finding information pointing to somebody else being guilty, or at least Justin being innocent, we'd learned that he'd been following the victim just a few hours before the murder. Talking about that with Col. Teal somehow made it even more depressing so that by the time our drinks arrived I wished I'd ordered something stronger than a light beer—like maybe a tankard of vodka.

We clinked our drinks and both took healthy swigs.

There really is a Bobbie McGee, and that's when I saw her. Bobbie dresses like a cowgirl, with wavy brown hair flowing out of her Stetson, and cultivates that persona. She also holds an MBA from the Wharton School of Business. Now in her mid-forties, she's been married for a decade to Brett McGee, the former Cincinnati Reds slugger.

"Hi, Bobbie!" I called her way. This was by way of a pre-emptive strike against yet another woman hailing me in friendly fashion in front of Lynda's father. Well known for the cordiality that added greatly to her establishment's popularity, she waved and came over to our table.

"How are you gents this evening?" From the professional look on her face as well as the rather robotic recitation of the words, I quickly realized that she had no idea who I was.

Humbled at my presumption in worrying that she would hail me first, I stood up and introduced myself. "I'm Jeff Cody, from St. Benignus. This is my future father-in-law, Col. Jake Teal."

Light dawned on her handsome features. "Oh, sure. Mac's brother-in-law! And you're marrying Lynda Teal. Congratulations!"

Of course she would know Sebastian McCabe. Everyone did. His "Friends" list on Facebook is nearing five thousand, which is dwarfed by his number of Twitter followers. Annoyed at only being remembered in connection to other people, I also saw an opening here. I stuck my foot in it.

"Thanks! I'm a very fortunate man." *Did you catch that, Colonel?* "Funny you should mention Mac. He wondered if you remember seeing this man in here last night."

I flashed my smart phone with the picture from Google Images.

"Oh, Lord, yes! That's the man who was shot. I recognized his face when I saw him on the noon news." She sat down. "How freaky is that? He was in here watching the news last night, and now he's on the news."

"About what time was it that he was here?"

"Cocktail hour ends at seven, and it was a little before that, so maybe 6:30 or 6:45." George Apple had said Kirtland had come back to Shamrocks & Ivy from his day of shopping around five o'clock. If he was anything like me, he would have taken a little down time before going out again for dinner. An hour and a half or so to nap, shower, read, and/or watch television seemed about right. The timetable was getting filled in nicely.

"Did you talk to him?" I asked.

"Just the usual. I stopped by his table and asked him if everything was okay. He said he was a little concerned about getting to the theater on time because his dinner hadn't come out yet. I promised to take care of it. I also ordered him a second drink on the house—he was having Old Ben Single Barrel, aged ten years. Good stuff!"

I was sure Lynda would have approved that attention to bourbon detail.

"Hey, can I freshen your glasses?" Bobbie added.

"Yes for me, no for him," Col. Teal said. I'd told him to not let me have a second beer and he'd come through. I made a mental note of his reliability.

Bobbie left us to put in the order. She passed Mindy on the way and filled her in. Our waitress had just taken our food order—baked fish for me, a steak sandwich for Lynda's father—when the smart phone buzzed. *Incoming!*

Not surprisingly, Lynda was texting a report from the bachelorette party: *She wants all my bridesmaids to dye their hair like mine!!!!* I was pretty sure "she" wasn't Triple M. A moment later she added a clarifying statement: *Mine is not dyed!* Sometimes Lynda had a whole different personality when she was texting.

I showed the text to the Colonel. "See what I mean? Your ex is driving Lynda crazy over this wedding."

He serenely sipped the last of his bourbon. "This isn't about the wedding, you know."

"Oh, really? You could have fooled me," I said bitterly. "I thought sure the band, the dress, and the bridesmaids all had something to do with the wedding."

"No, no, no, no. It's all about control. Lucia has to be in control. If she's not in control, she's not happy. And if Lucia's not happy, nobody's happy."

Was the beer getting to me or did that make perfect sense? Lynda only used the term "Mamma" when she wanted to irritate her mother. And yet her father, the non-custodial parent when she'd been growing up, she called "Daddy." But she hadn't talked much about him to me, the man she was going to marry. I don't know a lot about children of divorce; maybe all that was normal.

Mindy brought our plates ("Careful! They're hot!") and we tucked in.

"You know, Lynda really seems to like you," I ventured. I swallowed the last of my beer.

My companion looked up from his sandwich and raised his eyebrows. "What, that's a surprise? I'm a likeable guy, never mind that she's my daughter."

"It's just that she never talks about you, Jake."

And that's how it happened. Over food and drinks and family talk, I had slid without premeditation from "Colonel" mode into "Jake" mode. What did that mean? I have no idea. Ask my subconscious when you see it.

"It's complicated, son." *Now there's a phrase I know! It was my relationship status on Facebook for like six months.* "We always get along when I'm around. It's just that I haven't been around much during most of her life. Maybe it wasn't my fault—I like to think that it wasn't—but when she was a little girl who needed a father I was AWOL, off in some damned place she couldn't even pronounce much less locate on a map." He studied his empty bourbon glass. "She never talks about me, huh?"

"Well, she told me you were a colonel in the Army, but I didn't even know—"

DA-da-da-da—DA-da-da! The Indiana Jones theme song, the ring tone for all of my calls except those from Lynda (*Boléro*) and Ralph Pendergast (the Darth Vadar theme song), cut him off. I pulled out the phone and saw Mac's smiling face. "Excuse me," I said to Jake. "I'd better answer this. It's the Great Detective."

I touched the phone to pick up the call. "Shouldn't you be at the theater soon?"

"I already am, Jefferson. However, I have a few free moments. I believe it is time for a more extensive report of your day's activities, particularly the rather startling news that Justin followed his alleged victim on the day of the murder."

"Can I call you back in a few minutes? As you can hear, it's kind of noisy here at Bobbie McGee's. But we're almost finished."

"We?" Mac repeated. "Surely Ms. Teal is not—"

"No, she's not. I'm with Jake, her father." *Oops, I didn't mention that in my texts, did I?* "I'll explain later."

"Please do not tarry."

To save time, I didn't say goodbye before I touched the screen to disconnect the call. I had barely done so when a text from Lynda appeared on the screen:

Lucia hired male stripper!! Polly mortified, I'm ashamed. Everybody else embarrassed. Disaster!!!

I envisioned jaws dropping around Polly's modest apartment. (Exception: Popcorn more likely was drooling and possibly cheering.) This could not be ignored. But what was I supposed to do—send in the Marines?

No—the Army! That was it. I would send in the Army.

"Jake, here's your chance to be there for your daughter," I said. I read him the text. "I managed to get Lucia to back off once, but that was beginner's luck. Besides, I can't go to the bachelorette party, not even to stage a raid; that's against the rules of every wedding book or magazine ever published. So you need to ride to Lynda's rescue this time. As you said, it's never too late. Polly's apartment is less than a five-minute drive from here. I'll walk back to the B&B while you go over there and throw some clothes on that stripper."

This plan did not meet with the enthusiastic reception that I had hoped for.

"Lucia wouldn't take that well, son."

"But Lynda would! You'd be her hero. What are you afraid of? You're carrying a gun, for Pete's sake!"

"Two, actually." *Oh, great.* "But I couldn't shoot Lucia if my life depended on it." *That's a relief.*

I stood up. "I didn't really expect you to shoot anybody. All I meant was, you can handle this, Jake. There may be some yelling in Italian, but she probably won't hit you." The expression on his face made me think I'd assumed too much. "Well, anyway, it may not be easy and it sure won't be fun, but I know that in the end it'll be worth it." *I should have been a coach.*

"Oh, all right," Jake said. He stood up and headed out the door muttering, "But I wish you hadn't said, 'the end.' I don't like the sound of that."

Chapter Twenty-One
Bed and Restless

Sitting on the bed of my room at Shamrocks & Ivy, I called Mac back.

"So, how's the author-actor business going today?"

"Not particularly well," Mac responded in a muted tone, not at all like his normal buoyant self. "The curtain rises in less than two hours and we are still rehearsing Lafcadio's rewrites of my rewrites. Please report."

Trying to keep it concise, yet comprehensive, I started with Johanna Rawls. I left in the part about how I acquired my own sidekick, but skipped the details of the Teal family talk with the Colonel.

"The bottom line," I said in summation, "doesn't look good for Justin. I think I found out more than we want to know. Maybe I should have stayed at work today." *Work! I'd better check in with Popcorn and see what's going on even though it's after hours. No, wait, I can't. She's at that damned bachelorette party with her eyes bulging. Never mind, I'll catch up with her later.*

"Jefferson? Are you still there?"

"Yeah, sorry. The two gifts Kirtland bought yesterday—wine and jewelry—sure make it look like he was putting a full court press on Polly. Oscar's idea that Justin was jealous doesn't look a bit far-fetched. Even worse, Justin was stalking Kirtland just a few hours before Kirtland was murdered. I don't want to be the one to tell Polly this."

"Come now, old boy! The situation is nowhere near as dark for Justin as you seem to imagine. It is by no means certain, for example, that the earrings were intended for Polly. That is pure speculation."

"Does it really matter?" I shot back. "If Justin *thought* that Kirtland was running around buying presents for Polly, wouldn't that give him a reason to be jealous? We know Justin has a crush on Polly—she admitted that. I don't think that he was following Kirtland around town because he wanted to congratulate him or give him a few romantic pointers."

Mac took a moment to process that. "As to motive not being dependent on the reality of the situation, your observation is quite sound. Are we to believe, however, that this young man followed a professional detective for some time without being noticed?"

I shrugged, even though Mac couldn't see it. "Maybe Kirtland did notice and they had a confrontation that led to violence."

"I trust you mean 'led to violence *eventually*,' for any such confrontation certainly did not take place immediately before the murder."

"Okay, then, eventually," I said doggedly. "It's happened that way before. I remember the case of a Marine home on leave who got into a bar fight, went home, grabbed a rifle, and came back and killed the other guy. I don't know how he was able to argue lack of premeditation, but the judge only gave him five years.

"I'm not arguing that Justin did it, Mac. I'm just saying I don't think my day's work helped his cause any."

I smoothed out the amended timetable on my bed. I'd been scribbling on it all day long, adding names and refining times as if they actually meant anything. Mac might be able to keep it all in his head, but I couldn't. It now looked like this:

Timetable—Bill Kirtland's Last Day

8:00 A.M.	*Breakfast at Shamrocks & Ivy*
10:00 A.M.	*Polly's office*
11:00 A.M.	*Garrison's*
12:30 P.M.	*Daniel's with Polly*
1:45 P.M.	*Pages Gone By*
?	*Farmer's Market?*
2:30 P.M.	*Memories*
3:00 P.M.	*Other stores (possibly)*
3:30 P.M.	*Auld Lang Syne*
4:00 P.M.	*Act II*
4:30 P.M.	*Silk Stocking Winery*
5:00 P.M.	*Shamrocks & Ivy*
6:30 P.M.	*Bobbie McGee's*
7:40 P.M.	*Lyceum Theater*

Since this morning I had erased some question marks, added a few names of businesses and the estimated times Kirtland was there, and put a more realistic time to Kirtland's arrival at the theater for the eight o'clock performance. Other than that, I hadn't accomplished much. The times assigned were still about as fuzzy as that pair of dice wrapped around the rear view mirror on Mac's '59 Chevy.

"Those times I settled on, I wouldn't exactly call them arbitrary, but all the ones after lunch could go a half-hour or more in either direction," I said. "But it doesn't matter. There's no pattern. It doesn't add up to anything." Yes, I know that was three ways of saying the same thing. Before I taxed my creativity any further, Mac interrupted.

"On the contrary, old boy, the lack of a pattern does add up to something."

I hate it when he's being paradoxical.

"Try that again in singlespeak instead of doublespeak," I said.

"Perhaps it is too obvious for you to see it. Suppose you knew nothing about the individual whose activities are outlined on the timetable. What would you say about the way he spent his day?"

"I'd say he was killing time, wandering around from store to store like somebody on vacation or a two-day getaway."

"Precisely! He appears to have been without direction or purpose in his meanderings. And your interviews with shopkeepers and clerks point to the same conclusion. I am now certain that Bill Kirtland knew no one in Erin except Polly and that he had no mission here except to visit her. That is an important thing to know, and that is what your legwork has established. Well done, Jefferson!"

I was just metaphorically reaching over to pat myself on the back when Mac added, "Now, what was behind your comment that Kirtland had poor taste in literature?"

"Oh, that." Right on the heels of his compliment, I had to explain that my text had just been a smart-ass comment. "I was just kidding. He bought a used paperback of one of your yarns, said he's read it before."

"Which one?"

"*Hocus-Pocus.*"

"I wonder why that one? Pages Gone By has multiple copies of all of my books."

"Does there always have to be reason?"

"Not always. In my experience, however, there usually is."

The sound of Lafcadio Figg bellowing Mac's name in the background was my cue that the conversation was over. With a sigh, Mac promised to see me in the morning. He did, but under circumstances that neither of us could have imagined then.

Feeling hungry, I walked downstairs in search of a banana or an apple. House rules were that any food in the kitchen was available to guests. Pickings were slim, however, and I settled for two oranges.

Getting ready to mount the stairs, I heard the sound of the television in the parlor. I poked my head in. George Apple was sprawled out on the couch watching CNN Headline News. Some former African dictator had died in exile in Paris, a vigil was being held in Athens for the missing Cain child, and the Dow took a tumble after some recent gains (eroding a bit the value of my 403(b) retirement account).

We exchanged pleasantries.

"So, you're a play widower tonight?" I said.

"Yeah, it's the second night of the show. Hope it's less exciting than last night." We both laughed self-consciously.

"Have they cleaned out Bill's room yet?" *Now why did I ask that morbid question?*

George shook his head. "Cops · said I can't touch anything. I have to wait for the next of kin—a sister, I think. How did your day go?"

Not being the mix-and-mingle type, I really wanted to go back to my room and crash. But he looked lonely, so I sat down on a chair across from him and answered his endless questions about our efforts to help Justin. Having done this already with the even-more-probing Mac, the second time around was a snap.

"I think he did it," George said stubbornly when he'd finished grilling me. I didn't need to ask who *he* was.

From there we wandered into the more normal kind of conversation hosts and guests usually have on the first day of a B&B stay if one of the other guests didn't get murdered the night before. Business was so-so in this tight economy, George said. He and Sally had owned the house for eleven years.

"It took us two years to fix it up," he said.

Where was he from?

"Ann Arbor. I used to repossess cars for a living." I found that hard to believe. With his white hair and Col. Sanders goatee, I could imagine him selling cars more easily than I could picture him taking them back. I'd once known somebody who'd done the repossession thing for a living. He gave it up the night he got shot easing a delinquent owner's car out of his driveway at midnight.

"What brought you to Erin?" I asked.

"It was just luck, really. When Sally and I decided to open a B&B, we started looking in small Midwestern college towns. We figured that's the kind of place we'd like to live and there'd be a good trade in parents coming to check out the college or visit with their kids on weekends. Erin just happened to be where we found the right house."

As he started to go on about the history of the place, my phone broke out in Ravel's *Boléro*. Lynda was calling.

"Sebastian McCabe's assistant speaking," I said, standing up. "May I help you?"

With a wave of the two oranges in my right hand, I was already out of the parlor and climbing the steps to my room as Lynda ignored my witty sally and started talking.

"Daddy was awesome, Jeff! You should have seen him!"

"Did he make the stripper leave?"

"No, stripper was already gone. He finished up quickly and tastefully when he recognized Kate. Apparently he's one of her students in that drawing class she teaches on Tuesday nights. He was almost as embarrassed as I was. But Daddy swept up Lucia and took her with him. He was so masterful—like Tarzan! Daddy always was a man of action."

A man of action who carried a gun—make that, two guns. My brain cells were trying to make something out of that but they didn't know what.

"Of course my friends were all gaga over Daddy. He's so handsome!"

"Yes, indeed. Say, Lucia thinks I'm handsome, you know."

"Of course you are, darling."

"Well, it's a good thing I sent Jake over." *I mean, it was my idea. Give me a little credit here, Lyn.*

"He said something about that. What were you two doing together, anyway?"

So I told her about my day, strongly hinting that it had been very difficult and I could sure use a backrub. But apparently I was too subtle. Besides, the chef had just arrived at the bachelorette party—it was still early, after all—and it would have been rude of Lynda to leave. In fact, she had to get back to the party. So after a few expressions of undying love that are none of your business, I found myself off the phone and wondering what I was going to do with the rest of the evening.

First I ate the oranges.

Then I picked up *The Complete Sherlock Holmes* and opened it at random. "The Adventure of the Noble Bachelor" sounded promising. I'm noble and I would still be a bachelor for a couple more weeks, so I started reading. It turned out to be about some poor sap left at the altar on his wedding day. What kind of cruel chance led me to that story?

My mind wandered. I picked up the smart phone and started checking out the weather in our Italian honeymoon cities. That was a pleasant diversion, but it didn't last long. I looked at the television and decided I liked it better turned off.

I started thinking about the room below me, the one Bill Kirtland had stayed in. My private eye, Max Cutter, would pick the lock and have a look. Maybe Sherlock Holmes would, too! There could be a clue there, maybe something to help Justin. In a Max Cutter story, there *would* be a clue, although I had no idea what it would be.

Quietly, although George probably couldn't hear me over the sound of the television anyway, I snuck down the stairs and out the front door. Thanks to Daylight Savings Time, it was still light out. That was good and bad. Good because I could peek in the window of Bill Kirtland's first floor room, and bad because some nosey neighbor might catch me at it. Discounting the danger—I wasn't trespassing, after all—I walked around the side of the house, ducked when I passed the parlor in case George happened to look up from the TV, and stood outside the room the murder victim had occupied so briefly.

Not only did I not know how to pick the lock, I felt guilty just peering in the window. The blinds were open, giving me a surprisingly clear view of the room. It was about the same size as mine, with similar antique-store furnishings and decor— dresser with a mirror, hat stand, canopy bed. The fireplace had a painted black metal cover.

With sadness, I paid the most attention to what I could see of Bill Kirtland's personal effects. When he walked out of that room last night, not realizing that he would never be back, he had left behind him two suitcases (a large blue one showing its age and a smaller black one suitable for airline carry-on), a laptop computer, a shirt and a pair of pants folded over a wingback chair, and some purchases made in Erin. The bottle of wine, Mac's book, and a painted wooden chicken that he must have picked up at some craft store were neatly arrayed on the dresser.

Touched by the scene, I told myself to buck up and be professional. I took five photos with my smart phone, thankful for the adequate lighting, and immediately sent them to Mac. I was pretty proud of myself for sending him a visual report that translated to five thousand words, according to conventional wisdom. Mac might see the pictures tonight if he checked his e-mail after the performance. If not, tomorrow would be soon enough.

I snuck back up to my room and Sherlock Holmes. I decided to reread my favorite of those stories, "The Adventure of the Red-Headed League." I've actually read the whole book, although not fifty times like Mac, so I feel entitled to claim a favorite even though I don't remember every story. This is the one where the client's hair is as red as mine and Kate's. I began reading the first sentence: "I had called upon my friend, Mr.

Sherlock Holmes . . . " I stopped. There's another story that starts almost the same way. *I wonder if anybody's ever noticed that? Of course they have—those Sherlockians notice everything.* I resumed reading. I was barely through the opening scene in which Holmes makes all the deductions when I got an *incoming* on my phone. It was a text from my betrothed.

LYNDA: *I miss you.*

JEFF: *I can fix that.*

LYNDA: *mmm is staying with me tonight. She needs company.*

JEFF: *So do I.*

And so forth. The exchange was of a distinctly private nature that had nothing to do with the murder. Is it still called sexting if you're engaged?

Chapter Twenty-Two
Captured!

The next morning I turned the TV on while I dressed. The terrifying had gotten worse: CNN Headline News was reporting that police in Athens had found inconsistencies in the Cains' account of their son's disappearance. The parents were not cooperating with the investigation, police said. Meanwhile, a volunteer group that goes around the country aiding in searches for missing persons was searching the nearby woods for little Bart.

By the time I walked downstairs, I was once again in no condition to eat breakfast. The unimaginable thought that a parent would harm a child had made a mess out of my stomach. The alternative was also a nightmare: An innocent couple, anxious and frightened over the unexplained disappearance of their son, was now the object of suspicion. All keyed up, I decided that this was the morning to make up for the gym time I'd lost over the past few days. Too bad that didn't happen.

Amy Quong, looking more regal than anyone has a right to look in a Saturday morning pantsuit, was already at the breakfast table pouring her tea when I entered the dining room. Sally Apple was holding forth as she handed out plates of waffles and sausages (*"Laws are like sausages, it is better not to see them being made."—Otto von Bismarck.*)

". . . and Mr. Figg were still yelling at each other an hour before the play started," she was saying. "But Professor

McCabe delivered the new lines perfectly, even though he hated them."

"He's a trouper," I said, sitting down.

"Perhaps I should see this play," Amy Quong said, as if making a concession.

"Please do!" Sally said.

The Saturday edition of *The Erin Observer & News-Ledger* lay on the table in front of George, who was drinking coffee. The lead story was **A TALE OF TWO LIVES** by Johanna Rawls. It was the follow-up on the murder, what's known in the trade as the "second-day story." At a quick glance it looked as if Johanna had done a good job of packaging in one piece everything she could find out about the victim and the suspect, including some guarded comments from Triple M. But a quick glance was all I got.

DA-da-da-da—DA-da-da! I looked at the incoming phone number. It was blocked, and I don't like to answer blocked phone numbers, but I had a feeling that an eight o'clock Saturday morning call is one I shouldn't ignore. "Excuse me." Having never mastered the art of talking on the phone around a crowd of other people without being embarrassed, I left the room and walked into the parlor.

"Jeff Cody."

"Jeff? Jake." Before I could even process who that was—he'd only been Jake to me since that bottle of Hudy Delight at dinner last night—he went on: "I think you'd better get over here."

"You mean my apartment? What's wrong?" *Fire? Burglar? Squirrel invasion?* The unpleasant possibilities raced through my mind like a freight train.

"Nothing I can't handle, son. I have in front of me a skinhead with some ugly tattoos and body piercings. Sound familiar?"

Justin!

"I'd better call Mac."

144 Dan Andriacco

"I already did," Jake said. "Just get over here and join the party."

"Okay, I'll be right there. Don't let him get away."

"Are you kidding?" *Silly me.*

I stuck my head in the dining room and told them I had to go.

"But you didn't touch your breakfast!" Sally said. "Don't you want to eat? Or at least have some coffee?"

"I'd love to, but it's an office emergency."

Amy Quong regarded me skeptically. "On a Saturday morning?"

"Well, you know, the work never ends." Actually, this was true. Some of my most memorable media emergencies have happened on weekends, even if you don't count the ones involving homicide. Triple M's predecessor at Campus Ministries, for example, had gotten arrested on the Saturday before Christmas for punching out another woman during a brawl at a Wal-Mart store in Adams County. She had chosen to resign on the following Monday.

Between the B&B and my apartment above Mac's garage, I'm not sure the wheels of my bike touched the ground. I threw down the Schwinn and ran up the steps to the apartment.

Inside I found Col. Jake Teal and Justin facing each other in chairs. Jake was pointing a gun at the young man, who appeared about ready to throw up. He looked much more cowed than threatening, despite the tattoos and body piercings. Jake's steel gray eyes fixed him like a bayonet. Mac sat on my couch like a Buddha in a vast Sherlock Holmes Pub sweatshirt.

When Justin saw me, something like relief stole over his face. "I didn't do it, Mr. Cody!" *I've heard that before, Justin—right before you hung up on me.* He stood up in one swift, fluid movement.

"Careful, young man," Jake said. "My trigger finger has a mind of its own when faced with sudden moves."

Justin slowly sat down. "Tell him I didn't do it, Mr. Cody."

"I don't know that you didn't do it, Justin. You're going to have to convince me." I turned to Jake. "We'll have to call Oscar, but first—if you don't mind and it's not too much of a strain on you—please condescend to tell me *what the hell is going on here.*" I fear that my voice rose a little there at the end.

"I was walking back over here from Mac's house this morning when I saw him sneaking around. I knew who he was right away from the description."

"I wasn't sneaking around," Justin cried. "I was coming to turn myself in. I thought over what you said yesterday, Mr. Cody, and I decided it was the best thing to do. So I get here and I'm about ready to go up the steps and knock on your door when this guy sticks a gun in my back. What's with him, anyway?"

"He's retired," I explained. I turned to Jake. "I think you can put the gun away now. We've got him three to one." If Mac sat on him he would never get up. "What were you doing at Mac's house, anyway, Jake?" Sometimes I get stuck on inconsequential details.

"Never mind that. That doesn't matter." Jake holstered the gun inside his windbreaker.

Mac leaned forward, breaking his Buddha pose. "Justin, you have a lot of explaining to do."

"Should I call Polly?" I asked.

"Don't do that!" Justin said. "She'll kill me."

"And Johanna Rawls, too," I added. "We owe her one."

"I should like for Justin to answer a few questions before we call anyone, including the police. Where have you been, by the way, Justin?"

"With my friend Logan. But I ain't telling the cops that. I don't want him to get into no trouble, even though I think he was gonna kick me out anyway."

Mac nodded. "Your desire to protect your friend is understandable and even admirable." He pulled a cigar out of his shirt pocket beneath the sweatshirt. I was just glad he didn't pull it out of thin air; I hate it when he pulls magic tricks at serious moments. "However, I should strongly advise you to look out after your own interests while being totally candid and forthcoming with us. Let us begin with your relationship with the deceased. We know that Polly introduced you to him at the theater. Was that the first time you saw him?"

"Yes."

"Was it the last?" Mac knew the answer to that, of course; it was a test question.

"No. He almost choked me yesterday afternoon."

"Oh, this is going to be good!" Jake said with a gleam in his eye.

Mac shot him a *shut up* look, and then turned back to Justin. "Why don't you start by telling us why you were following him?"

"How did you . . ." His eyes looked like those of a trapped rat. He swallowed and decided the question was useless. "I didn't like the way he looked at Sister Polly. I was worried about her. She's kind of innocent, you know." She was about ten years older than Justin and a veteran of the U.S. Army, but I kept that to myself. "I thought he was up to no freaking good, so I decided to follow him and see. I guess it was dumb idea." *No argument there, Justin!*

"He went to that winery out on the highway and bought a bottle of wine. I even heard him mention the name 'Polly.' So I kept following him to this old house. I guess it's where he was staying. I sat there for a while, waiting for him to come out the front door but he must have come out the back and circled around because the next thing I knew my back door flew open and this arm was around my neck." He mimicked the attack with his own right arm. "He said something like, 'Okay, pal, game's over.' I thought he was going to kill me. I really had a bad day Thursday." *Not as bad as Bill Kirtland, kid.* "Then he said, 'Wait a minute. What the hell! You're that friend of Polly's.' It was like he was expecting me to be somebody else."

Mac looked like the cat that ate the canary and followed it up with salmon for dessert. "Now that is significant, by thunder! Whoever Kirtland thought you were may have been the one who killed him. What else did he say about that person?"

"Nothing. We weren't exactly buddies, you know. He asked me what the eff I thought I was doing. I told him I was watching out for Sister Polly, that she's a good person and he shouldn't be messing with no nun. He . . . he laughed at me at first. Then he said, 'I guess you're okay, kid. Dumb, but okay.' I didn't like that, that's why I remembered it. Then he said, 'I wasn't messing with her. We knew each other a long time ago. I just wanted to be sure that she's happy, and now I know that she is.' He got out of my car and told me never to do a stupid thing like that again. Then he leaned in and said, 'She's lucky to have a friend like you, and you're lucky to have a friend like her, so don't screw it up.' And then he told me I could go. That's the last I seen of him alive. Can I have a cigarette now?"

"No," I said. "Nobody smokes in my apartment."

Mac waved his unlit cigar as if to verify the statement. "Tell us about seeing him dead, Justin. How did that happen?"

"It's just like I told Chief Hummel. I went out behind the theater to grab a smoke and I saw this body. At first I didn't know what it was, and then when I realized it was a person I didn't recognize him. He looked different dead, all messed up and wearing different clothes. When I heard you and the chief talking and you said who it was, I freaked out. I knew I'd be in trouble. So I ran."

"Guilty conscience," Jake observed. "If you'd stayed put, you might never have been a suspect."

Maybe, maybe not. I'd found out that Justin was following Kirtland, and I'm no Max Cutter. So that fact might have come out and cast suspicion on Justin. But it was pointless to speculate on what might have been, so I changed the subject.

"Kirtland was facing the back of Market Street," I pointed out. "Do you have any idea what he might have been looking at?"

Justin shrugged, making the snakes on his forearms wiggle. "How should I know?"

"I want you to think back to when you were in the theater, backstage, and you decided to go outside," Mac said. "From that point to the point where you saw the body, did you see anything out of the ordinary—anything at all? Do not make any judgments about how important it might be. We can sort that out later. Think hard."

Justin appeared to concentrate, scrunching his pierced eyebrows. After a while, he said, "It's no use. I don't remember nothing unusual. There were a lot of people running around in back, but they didn't need me. I worked on building the sets. So I figured Sister Polly wouldn't notice if I snuck out for a few minutes to grab a smoke."

That hung in the air a while as nobody seemed to have anything else to ask.

"I hate to break up the party," Jake said finally, "but shouldn't we call the cops—like about twenty minutes ago?"

He should have done that before calling us, legally speaking, but I'm glad he didn't.

"Of course," Mac said, meaning he was finished interrogating Justin, at least for now. "I shall call Oscar and let him know that his person of interest came to us and surrendered of his own free will. I do not think we have to mention Col. Teal's unfortunate misperception about Justin's presence here. Are we all agreed, gentlemen?"

We were.

Mac called Oscar and I called Johanna and Triple M— over Justin's protests—and asked them to meet us at the jail. "I'm at Lynda's apartment," Triple M said, "but I'll be right there." In the background, I heard, "I'm coming along!" Who was I to discourage my beloved whom I hadn't seen in person since that dust-up in her office? Johanna didn't answer her cell phone, so I left a message.

Before the four of us piled into Mac's boat-sized Chevy, I managed to get in a few words with him in private.

"So what do you make of the idea that Kirtland thought Justin was somebody else—somebody he was willing to practically choke at first sight?" I asked.

"I think it has great promise, old boy. I have no doubt that Justin was telling the truth. He simply does not have the imagination to invent that scene. Our challenge is to discover who Kirtland was expecting or fearing."

There was one other thing, a tiny detail that still bugged me.

"What was Jake doing at your house this morning?"

"He never left it after bringing Lucia home from the bachelorette party last night," Mac said. "I had trouble sleeping because of all the noise they were making—last night when I came home from the theater, and then again this morning."

"You mean they were fighting all night?"

"That was not the kind of noise they were making, Jefferson."

TMI! TMI! I think I might have blushed. "Oh. Well. So how did the play go?"

"The script changes were not to my liking, but the audience seemed appreciative," Mac conceded.

It takes a big man to admit he might have been wrong, and Sebastian McCabe is certainly a big man.

Chapter Twenty-Three
The Right to Remain Silent

Justin seemed increasingly nervous on the short car ride to the jail. Who could blame him? I just wasn't sure whether he was more nervous about hearing the jail door clink behind him or about having to face Sister Polly, as he called her.

As the four of us got out of the Chevy in front of City Hall, with Jake's hand on Justin's arm in a seemingly friendly embrace, I was suddenly struck by the chilling fear that Oscar had called TV4 or one of the other Cincinnati TV stations to get video of the event. I wouldn't put it past him, friend or no friend.

But it didn't happen. We walked into the Civil War-era building and down the steps to the city jail and Oscar's basement office without incident. The room was tight for five people, especially when two of them were Mac and Oscar.

Oscar had put on his uniform with the official hat and his most solemn expression for the occasion. I was impressed by his businesslike demeanor as he got up from his green desk and came over to meet us. He nodded to Mac and me, which seemed both a silent thanks for bringing in the fugitive and an assumption of custody. I broke the mood a bit by introducing Jake as Lynda's father. Oscar pronounced himself pleased to meet him, then turned to Justin.

"Justin Bird," he intoned, "you have the right to remain silent. Anything you say or do can and will be held against you in a court of law. You have the right to speak to an attorney. If you cannot afford an attorney, one will be appointed for you. Do you understand these rights?"

Justin looked at me, his face a question mark.

"This is just like TV," I explained. "He wants to ask you questions, but you don't have to talk to him without a lawyer unless you want to. If you don't have the money to pay for a lawyer"—that was a safe bet—"you can get what's called a public defender at no charge."

"What should I do?"

Shut up!

"I am sure you wish to cooperate to the best of your ability," Mac said. "However, even though you are innocent of any wrongdoing whatsoever, legal representation would be in your best interests. I shall be pleased to secure the services of Erica Slade on your behalf."

That was bringing in the big guns. Erica Slade may not be a nationally known defense attorney, like Aristotle O'Doul or someone of that stature, but here in Sussex County she is hell on wheels. She particularly enjoys fighting with the county prosecutor, something she apparently got practice at during the six years they were married. A former gym teacher and Cincinnati Bengals cheerleader, she has also occasionally been accused of overdressing for court. The courthouse wags like to say that her stiletto heels and her legal acumen are equally sharp.

"But I already told you everything I know," Justin said to Mac.

Eyes bulging out almost as far as his stomach, Oscar exploded with an impressive stream of curses. I had no idea his vocabulary could be so colorful. After the windup, he threw the pitch: "This time you've gone too damned far, Mac. That's witness tampering! I'll have your hide!"

That was quite an image, Mac's hide being the size it is. But Mac chuckled, all good-natured bonhomie. "Do not be ridiculous, Oscar! Witness tampering is the crime of attempting to coerce or intimidate a witness in a federal trial. So far as I am aware, Justin Bird has not been summoned to be a witness in any trial, much less a federal one, nor did I try to coerce him."

"Well, then," Oscar said heavily, "if it's not that, it's something else!"

Jake tried hard to stifle a smile, hiding his mouth behind his right hand.

Mac showed his palms, a pleading gesture. "What, pray tell? Of what am I culpable? You wished to speak to Justin regarding a murder most foul. My associates and I brought him to you so that you could do so. I am unaware of any law that would require him to remain silent in the interim, or that would require us to plug our ears if he wished to speak to us."

That was a lot of hooey, of course. Mac made it sound like Justin had insisted on blabbing and practically forced us to listen. As to the legal part, I didn't know whether Mac was just blowing smoke or not—but I could tell that Oscar didn't either. He pulled open the desk drawer where he keeps his cigarettes for emergencies, looked mournfully at the emptiness within, and slammed it shut. He looked longingly at the bulge in Justin's shirt pocket.

While he was trying to figure out whether it was ethical to try to cadge a cigarette out of a suspect, in came Lynda and the jail's volunteer chaplain, Sister Mary Margaret Malone. Neither looked well rested, although Triple M wasn't as baggy-eyed as she had been the day before. She was dressed in a blue sweater and khaki slacks. Lynda's naturally curly hair hung wet, as if she had just stepped out of the shower (a fetching prospect). Normally a dresses and skirts girl, she was clad in an Orange Zebra concert T-shirt, which she filled out quite nicely, and a pair of cut-off shorts that I presumed to be the closest clothes handy when the phone rang.

Before I could even say hi, Triple M immediately ran over to Justin. "Are you all right?"

"Yes, Sister." Boy, did that bring back memories! I learned to say "Yes, Sister" by reflex through eight grades of St.

Polycarp School in Williamsburg, Virginia. And I wasn't even Catholic at the time.

She held his hands in hers, speaking in a low voice as if she were gentling a wild animal.

In the ten seconds it took that to happen, nobody moved. I turned around and realized that Lynda was looking from Jake to me as if she didn't know whom to approach first. Jake was standing right next to me, so I stepped back. With a grateful glance at me, Lynda hugged her father and thanked him for saving her bachelorette party. He grinned modestly. Then I got my turn for a hug, but I wasn't going to settle for that.

"It's kind of crowded in here," I whispered. "Let's step out for a minute."

We ducked into a deserted hallway—it was a Saturday, after all—and smooched a bit. Her freshly shampooed hair gave off a delightful flowery smell. The activities of the last few days had seriously cut into our engaged-couple time and I'd missed the closeness.

"So, how's Mom?" I asked when we came up for air, just to get the conversational ball rolling.

Speaking of rolling, Lynda rolled her eyes in a familiar *good grief!* gesture. "I haven't seen her this morning, thank heavens."

"She must have been otherwise occupied." If Lynda didn't know how, I wasn't going to enlighten her.

"Her latest brainstorm—before the stripper went into action—was a butterfly release in the church just after we exchange our vows."

That didn't sound *that* bad. "Maybe you ought to compromise, throw her a bone."

The way Lynda stared at me, you'd have thought that I'd suddenly grown an extra couple of heads. "Are you out of your mind? How does one compromise with a butterfly release?"

What am I, the wedding planner? "I don't know. Limit it to two butterflies maybe?" Blessed with an impeccable sense of timing, I decided to shift gears. "I called Johanna to let her know about Justin turning himself in. She didn't answer, but I left a message."

"You're a good man, Jeff Cody." Apparently that was worth another hug. "How would you like to have dinner at my place tonight?"

Be still my beating heart.

"I'll see if I can fit you into my crowded—"

"Jefferson!" Mac stood in the formerly empty corridor. "Oh, am I intruding? I apologize. Erica has agreed to represent Justin. She is on her way. You and I have better things to do than to wait for her to arrive, however. Another line of inquiry has suggested itself to me."

Nettled as I was at Mac's interruption of the promising tête-à-tête with my wife-to-be, my curiosity got the best of me.

"And what 'line of inquiry' would that be, oh Great Detective?"

"Why did Kirtland leave the theater during the performance?" Mac said, ignoring my sarcasm as usual. "That has been a significant question from the beginning, of course. Now I am beginning to suspect that it may have had something to do with this mysterious unknown person for whom Kirtland mistook Justin. And who might be able to shed light on Kirtland's premature departure?"

"Somebody working the concessions," Lynda said.

Mac's eyebrows did calisthenics, an unusual display of surprise for him. He usually raises just one eyebrow. Surprised myself, I turned to Lynda.

"Well," she said, as if defending herself, "I just thought that on his way out he might have said something that one of the people selling the candy and drinks heard. Or maybe they even saw something."

"That is precisely what I was thinking!" Mac thundered. "Clearly, Lynda, you have some untapped Sherlockian impulses. Perhaps you would like to accompany us on this venture?"

She'd done it before, with me, but that was when she was in her reporter mode. She shook her head. "I think I'd better scoot over to your house, Mac, and talk to my mother. After that imbroglio last night at my bachelorette party I'd like to make peace before the wedding—especially between her and my father."

"That might not be so hard," I said.

Chapter Twenty-Four
A Call for Murder

"So where are we going?" I asked Mac as we left City Hall.

"We are taking a brief walk to the main branch of the public library. Carl Petermann, the head of the fiction desk, is a member of the Lyceum Players and was part of the concession stand team on Thursday night. Of the three volunteers working there that night, I judge him to be the most observant and the most reliable witness."

"What's going to happen next for Justin?"

"I suspect that by now he has given Oscar one of his cigarettes, but will not smoke in Polly's presence, which I find rather endearing."

"Yeah," I agreed, "he's cute as a button. But I was more wondering whether he's going to talk to Oscar and whether he's going to spend the night in jail."

Mac shook his head. "I find both scenarios unlikely. Erica will argue, quite rightly, that she needs time to meet with her client and familiarize herself with his case before he submits to an interview. Lawyers are seldom in a hurry. I suspect that she will make an appointment with Oscar for Monday, calendar permitting. Meanwhile, Oscar certainly has no real evidence to give the prosecutor for a suspicion of murder charge."

"What about fleeing the scene?"

"He came back of his own volition. No, I do not think Justin's freedom is at risk for at least a few days. I expect that he and our other friends will be gone by the time we drop in on

Oscar again later. The chief has an appointment with Bill Kirtland's sister at eleven o'clock and I would like to meet her."

I stared at Mac. "Uh, did you happen to notice that Oscar is furious at you for calling in Erica Slade and telling Justin to clam up?"

"Correction," Mac said. "He is no longer. I rectified that while you and Ms. Teal were canoodling. First, I pointed out to him that it is to his benefit for Justin to have an attorney present so that any information secured in the interview is usable in whatever case might develop from it. In other words, he need not fear the dreaded cliché 'tossed out on a technicality.'"

"And Oscar bought that?" I was incredulous.

"Not without difficulty, but yes. Further, I assured Oscar on my honor as a fellow Hibernian and a magician that in our conversation Justin denied culpability in Bill Kirtland's death and that I found him credible. Oscar believed me, even if he did not believe what Justin told me. Therefore, he knows that an interview with Justin is unlikely to yield a confession, with or without an attorney present. Hence, he was no longer cursing at me by the time I left his company."

I swear that my brother-in-law could sell sand to the Saudis and make a profit at it.

"If you think Justin's story is so believable, why don't you let him tell it? Why bring in the defense lawyer that the prosecutor hates the most—his ex-wife?"

Mac sighed. "Though you may find this hard to credit, Jefferson, my confidence in my own abilities is not unbounded. If we are not successful in finding the real killer, Justin may have to stand trial even though I believe that the case against him at this point is singularly weak. If that happens, I want to be sure that he has the best possible legal representation from the beginning. Ah, here we are."

The main branch of the Public Library of Erin and Sussex County is a brick and stone Andrew Carnegie affair that has been added to several times over the past hundred years.

With parking lots, it takes up most of a block on Mulberry Street.

We found Carl Petermann behind a curved desk on the balcony level. He was a little older than me, say early forties. While the top of his head was bald as an egg, bushy gray-brown hair sprouted at the sides, like it was held in place by his thick horn-rim glasses. He was wearing a short-sleeved white shirt and a necktie held in place with a silver clip in the shape of an open book.

"Good morning, Mac." The librarian's moon face split into a pleasant smile as he hailed us. Mac did the introductions. As Petermann reached out to shake my hand, I noticed that his right wrist was tattooed with a blue ". I wondered whether he had a " on the left.

Mac quickly brought him up to speed on why we were there.

"Yeah, sure, I remember," Petermann said. "I've been thinking about it ever since I heard about the murder. I figured that must have been the victim I saw leaving the theater in such a hurry with a cell phone pressed to his ear. He caught my attention because, first of all, I loathe cell phones, and secondly, I've been to enough plays to know that people just don't walk out that late in a show. If they don't like it, they leave before or during the intermission."

"Presumably he had the phone in 'vibrate' mode during the performance," Mac mused. "Nevertheless, he responded to an incoming call—perhaps one luring him to his death."

"Well, that would make sense," I said.

Mac raised an eyebrow.

"I mean, when I saw his body there was a cell phone just inches away from his right hand," I explained. "He must have been either talking on his phone or taking a picture when he died." I stopped, struck by what I'd just said. "Hey, we wondered what he was looking at when he died. Maybe he took a picture of it!"

"Or maybe he was still talking on the phone," Mac said. "This is highly significant. Hell and damnation, Jefferson, why did no one tell me that Kirtland's cell phone may have been in use when he was killed?" *Uh, I guess because we didn't think of that.* "I saw the phone among the items on his body, but I assumed it had been in his pocket like any good cell phone during a play."

Petermann blinked. "So is what I told you important?"

"Indeed, it could be vital," Mac said.

"Cool! I'm a big mystery fan, you know. It's my favorite leisure reading."

"The only thing better would be if you happened to hear what Kirtland was saying as he left the theater."

"I wasn't eavesdropping," Petermann huffed. "Besides, he was talking in a low voice."

Mac thanked Petermann for his help. We turned to leave—and almost ran smack into the stocky frame of Lafcadio Figg. The last week had not been kind to the retired teacher. His long gray hair was tangled and greasy, his mutton chops overdue for a trimming. He looked like he'd slept in his suit.

"Lafcadio!" Mac's hearty conviviality rang hollow. He bowed. Can one bow ironically? "How nice to see you in the library! If you are looking for Sherlock Holmes books, you will find them shelved under 'D' for Doyle."

Wow, I wouldn't slam a door that hard.

"Oh, I'm here to pick up your latest mystery novel, Sebastian."

"Really?" For my brother-in-law, a response like that amounted to being nearly speechless.

"Yes," Figg said. "I never buy them, you know. I presume I'll find it shelved under A for—"

"Congratulations, Lafcadio," I interrupted loudly. "Nine months ago the Lyceum Theater was just a dream. The skeptics thought you would never be able to buy the theater, much less fix it up, start a theatrical company, and mount your first production all within less than a year. You've done it all!"

"Well, thank you." For a moment, I thought he was going to let it rest there, but reality got the better of him. "Let's just say so far, so good. If we can pack the house again next weekend, I'll call it a success."

"It already is," Petermann said. He leaned forward from his curved desk. Yep, both wrists were tattooed. "The whole town's talking about it. I bet you'll find some foundation money coming forward now that we're in business."

With Carl Petermann and me both lauding Lafcadio Figg, piling on the plaudits, Mac almost had to say something. But what he said surprised the heck out of me.

"My friends are right, Lafcadio. Your achievement with the Lyceum Theater and the Lyceum Players is nothing short of remarkable. And I feel confident that it will continue. Congratulations indeed!" He put out his hand. After a moment of stunned silence, Figg accepted warily, as if he were afraid Mac had a buzzer in his palm. (He didn't.) The two old rivals shook hands. It had the air of a handshake before a boxing match, but it was still a handshake.

"Come along, Jefferson!"

I was only too happy to get out of there before Mac and Figg reverted to their usual fighting form.

"Well, that was big of you," I told Mac, "shaking his hand and all."

"I wanted to see if his hand was sweating. It was."

"What does that mean?"

"Perhaps nothing. However, it is an interesting fact."

"You and Figg are quite a pair, like Gilbert and Sullivan. I guess that's what they call creative differences."

"I am not sure how creative it is," Mac said, "and I wonder what Lafcadio was really doing in the library."

Chapter Twenty-Five
Sole Survivor

Sometimes a trip to the library is just a trip to the library, I thought as we hoofed it back to City Hall and Oscar's dungeon. And my hand would be sweating, too, after a verbal joust with Sebastian McCabe! We walked mostly in silence. While Mac was thinking Great Thoughts, I was wondering how Lynda was handling her mother.

When we arrived back at the lower level of City Hall, we found Johanna Rawls pacing back and forth outside of Oscar's office. Even in tennis shoes she was what my grandfather would have called "a tall drink of water." With that straight platinum hair and slim figure, she looked like a travel poster for Sweden.

When she saw us, she walked our way.

"Jeff! Thanks for calling me about Justin," she said. "I'm sorry I missed you. I was out for my morning run. I got here as soon as I could."

"So, did you talk to Justin?"

"Not exactly. He was just leaving with his lawyer." I stole a glance at my companion, whose fault that was. "But I already know Erica Slade. I'm pretty sure I can get something useable out of her for the Sunday paper. I'll call her in a couple of hours and remind her of what I told her, that I went to high school with Justin and we have mutual friends, sort of."

"And meanwhile," Mac said, "you still hope to find a story in these hallowed halls as well."

It didn't take a Sherlock Holmes to observe that Johanna had a cell phone in one hand and a reporter's notebook in another, as well as a purse slung over her shoulder. She was loaded for journalistic bear.

"The victim's sister is in there with Oscar," Johanna said. "I'm waiting to get a crack at her."

"Of course," Mac said. "Oscar told us she was coming in this afternoon. We are hoping to speak with her ourselves. Come along, Jefferson."

Despite the McCabe self-confidence, I myself wasn't so sure what kind of reception we would receive after Mac's pesky insistence that Justin get lawyered up. But I figured I could always duck.

The woman sitting in the chair in front of Oscar was about Lynda's age, thirty-ish, with flowing dark hair. The resemblance to Bill Kirtland was unmistakable in her nose and jaw line. Her eyes were puffy and her makeup smeared. She held a crumpled tissue in her right hand. When she stood up upon our entrance, I saw that she was wearing skinny black jeans, stylish but well worn, below her light blue blouse and denim jacket.

Oscar did not stand up.

He looked at Mac with a sour expression. "If you tell her to get a lawyer, too, I'm gonna kick your big ass right out of here."

"Oscar, you wound me." Mac looked wounded. "As you well know, my only intention is to serve the cause of justice, as I have done even when the consequences were personally painful." That wasn't even a slight exaggeration. He had once fingered a friend for murder and I had seen the sadness in his eyes. "I am quite sure that no legal representation is necessary for—" He cocked a quizzical eyebrow.

"This is a Mary Rose Kirtland," Oscar said.

"My name is Sebastian McCabe." He bowed at her. "This is Thomas Jefferson Cody. You have our sincere sympathy on your brother's tragic passing."

"I'm sorry, I don't quite understand your role here?" She ended the sentence on an upnote, as if it were a question instead of a statement.

"We're kind of like consultants," I said.

Oscar sat back, as if undecided how to play it.

"We helped the chief solve some other murders," I added.

Apparently that decided it. "Ms. Kirtland was just telling me a bit about her brother," Oscar said. "They were pretty close. Their parents are dead and she's his sole survivor. She said he'd never been married—dated a little in recent years, but nothing serious."

Mary Rose Kirtland sat down, and so did Mac and I.

"I don't think he ever really got over Polly, the girl he dated in the Army," she said. "I understand she lives here. I'd like to see her again, make sure she knows how much Bill cared for her."

I think she knows.

"Forgive the obvious question," Mac said, "but did your brother have any enemies that you know of?"

She gave a wan smile. "He's been—had been—a private detective almost since he got out of the Army. I imagine there are a few errant husbands that he might have pissed off. But I don't know of any threats or anything like that.

"He didn't get along very well with my ex?" Again that uplift at the end of the sentence. "He was angry with Frank for leaving me and our three kids for another man, and for being chronically late with child support payments. But Frank is just irresponsible—he wouldn't deliberately harm a butterfly."

"Seeing as how your brother wasn't a butterfly," Oscar said, "I'd better take his name and contact info just for the record."

So she gave him the name, Frank Lamprey, his address, and three phone numbers.

"Do you know much about your brother's business?" Mac asked.

"I know almost everything about it. I kept the books for him. It was a part-time job on top of my nine-to-five— actually, it was an excuse for him to help me out as much as anything? He was five years older than me and always trying to take care of me, even all those years when he was in the Army. His PI work wasn't as exciting as you might think from watching television. He used websites and social media a lot more than he used a gun." She shook her head. "You'd be amazed at the self-inflicted wounds people deliver with their Facebook and Twitter postings."

No, I wouldn't.

"But he did carry a gun," I pointed out. "He had one on him when he was shot." I thought of what Jake had said about professionals carrying a second gun. "Did he carry a backup?"

"You mean another gun?" I nodded. She thought about it. "I guess he could have. I know he had a couple of guns. I don't know anything about those things, I hate them, but one was his Army weapon and the other was a Walther."

"That's the kind of gun that I think killed your brother, a Walther PPK/S .380, based on the cartridges," Oscar said. "When you get into his room at the B&B, will you let me know whether a Walther is among his effects?"

"Of course. I have to pick up his Fusion, his suitcase, whatever. You're thinking he might have been shot with his own weapon?"

"Coincidences tend to get my attention, that's all," Oscar said.

"Could you tell us about your brother's current cases?" Mac asked.

She swept her hair out of her eyes. "I suppose it wouldn't hurt to talk about them in general. I mean, I can't give you details, like the name of clients. That wouldn't be ethical.

"Bill had four active cases. The oldest was an insurance case where he was trying to find a bank embezzler named Allison Lee—that one's a public case and her picture is even on wanted posters, so I can tell you that. He was also investigating the background of a fiancé for a very nervous father of the bride-to-be and looking into reports of corruption on a military contract. Then just in the last few days something new come up—so hush-hush he wouldn't even tell me anything about it."

"Nothing at all?" I pressed.

"I just knew that the client was local? He had clients from all over, but Bill drove out to meet this one and he wasn't gone long."

"I am intrigued by the background check on the fiancé," Mac said. "I am sure that many future fathers-in-law have doubts about their daughter's choice of mate." *Doubts? What's to doubt? Daughter knows best.* "However, few would go to the lengths of hiring a private investigator unless they had a lot of money or grave suspicions. Either way, it interests me. I understand your unwillingness to give us the client's name. However, perhaps the client would have no such hesitation. Would you be willing to contact him and ask his permission?" Mac handed her a business card with his contact information.

"If it might help find my brother's killer, of course I'd be glad to," she said, taking the card. "But I understood you had a suspect?"

"I believe 'person of interest' would be the correct term," Mac said, looking at Oscar.

"I would even say he's a person of a great deal of interest," the chief added. He glanced at me, perhaps remembering the time he had auditioned me for the role of jealous killer. "But it's still early. We don't want to jump to any hasty conclusions."

He pulled open his desk drawer, withdrew a big manila envelope, and poured the contents on the table.

"These are the personal effects that were on your brother when he was killed," Oscar said. It was all the stuff we'd seen before—keys, gun, Swiss Army knife, watch, wallet, the little box, the smart phone.

"Have you checked the phone?" Mac asked.

"For what?"

"For the record of incoming calls. I will be frank." He opened his hands in a frank gesture. Right away I figured Mac was going to try to pull the wool over Oscar's eyes, but he fooled me by playing it straight. "We just spoke with Carl Petermann, who was working at the Lyceum's concession stand on the night of the murder. He told us that Bill Kirtland was talking on a cell phone when he left the theater that night. Whomever he was talking to is at the least an important witness, perhaps even a murderer. I am confident it was not Justin Bird, incidentally."

That last part wasn't hard to figure—Justin wouldn't likely be calling him for a chit-chat after Kirtland almost throttled him not long before. But then Mac was reasoning from the assumption that Justin was no killer. Maybe that was right, maybe not.

"And also check for relevant photos," Mac said. "Mr. Kirtland may have taken a picture of whatever he was looking at when he was killed."

"Any other orders?" Oscar said sourly, pointedly putting the phone to one side.

Mac might have given him some if Oscar hadn't handed Mary Rose Kirtland the box and an explanation. "This was in his coat pocket. He bought 'em here in town."

She opened the box, saw nestled inside it the unusual jade earrings with the rose design, and immediately began crying. She covered her face with what remained of her tissue. I wanted to pat her on the back or something, but I didn't know about the protocol for that. How do you comfort somebody you'd just met? There must be people who do that all the time—doctors, paramedics, cops, and such—but I am not among them.

"Those earrings had to be for me," she managed to say between sniffs. "On his last day he was thinking of his little sister. He always did that when he was out of town—brought me back roses of some kind because of my name. He always called me his little rose."

Chapter Twenty-Six
Checkmate

"Oh, it's adorable!" Lynda said. She held out the colorful enamel parrot pin I'd bought her at Auld Lang Syne. "What's the occasion?"

"A date with my fiancée. Lately, that qualifies as a special occasion. I'm glad you like it."

She pinned it to her ample bosom, gently declining my offer of help. It looked good against her bright yellow blouse. In my head I could hear the raspy voice of Maisie Weisgerber saying, "Don't settle."

We stood on the back deck of the second-floor apartment where Lynda would be living for just a couple more weeks. She was grilling us chicken and corn, letting me turn the corn once in a while just to feel useful. It was a meal perfect for Memorial Day, but by then we'd be in Italy on our honeymoon. The sun was playing peek-a-boo, in and out of the clouds, but the temperature was in the 70s.

I picked up my can of caffeine-free Diet Coke and clinked it against her Knob Creek Manhattan in a frosted cocktail glass. "Cheers." We sat next to each other in fabric and aluminum chaise lounges.

"So how did it go today with the luscious Lucia?" I asked.

Lynda closed her eyes and stretched out her long legs, fully enjoying the moment as she sipped her cocktail. She was wearing a white tennis skirt with polka dots. "Not bad. She was in a good mood."

"I wouldn't be surprised if she were downright mellow."

My betrothed regarded me suspiciously. I almost broke down and told her about Mac's sleepless night, but nobody wants to hear that about her parents. It's icky, to use Lynda's word. I tried to look innocent.

"I followed your suggestion and compromised," Lynda said. "We're going to have a butterfly release outside of the church, as we process out after the wedding."

"Beautiful." I meant it.

"And I said it was okay if she supplied some additional flowers."

"That doesn't sound so over-the-top."

"She's having them flown in from Hawaii. How was your day?"

Answering that question took us through most of dinner. I had to start from the beginning because I hadn't had a chance to fill her in on her father holding Justin at gunpoint— she didn't seem shocked—and Justin's account of his interview with Bill Kirtland. From there I proceeded chronologically through everything that she hadn't witnessed herself. Because I'd decided to give her the complete treatment, I described the whole library episode from Carl Petermann's " " tattoos to Mac's enigmatic pondering what Figg was up to at the library.

"Do you think Mac really suspects Figg of something illegal, immoral, or otherwise underhanded?" she asked.

"I think he did at the time. Of course, that may have just been motivated by pique. This is Sebastian McCabe we're talking about, after all."

Over dessert of strawberries, blueberries, and Cool Whip Lite, I described our encounter with Mary Rose Kirtland. This brought me to the summary:

"So we know that Bill Kirtland still cared about Polly, but he wasn't bringing her romantic gifts—just an innocent bottle of wine. According to Justin's account, Kirtland said that he visited her just because he wanted to be sure she was happy. And he seemed convinced that she is."

"If Justin believed all that, he had no reason no kill Bill," Lynda pointed out.

"Well, no romantic reason. I suppose he could have been really irked about Kirtland sneaking up behind him and choking him. But I don't think Erica Slade's ex would want to go to trial offering that as a motive. So, on balance, I guess it was a good day for Justin, although the whole following-Kirtland thing is going to look bad if it comes out. At least he's got a lawyer, and a damned good one, to help him through it. And she can claim he willingly turned himself in, which is even sort of true."

Lynda shook her honey-colored curls. "Poor Polly. What a mess for her to get mixed up in!"

"How's she taking it?"

"You know her—she's always upbeat. Still, it's been difficult. In a small town, there's always talk." *The male stripper at her apartment should be good for a few days' gossip.* I didn't say that out loud, but it was damned hard not to.

"Have you heard anything about how the other sisters are reacting?" I asked.

"Polly's community has been very supportive. They're a great bunch of women. Heck, if it hadn't been for you, I might have joined them."

I chuckled politely. Then I noticed that Lynda wasn't chuckling. In fact, she was looking at me as if I'd committed a faux pas.

"What? What did I do?" Then it dawned on me. "You're serious, aren't you?" *No flies on me.*

"Yeah, I gave it a lot of thought at one point."

"When was this?" I was thinking maybe high school, college.

"Last year, around March, early April."

That was somewhere between Lynda's "Let's be friends" speech and our reconnecting over a dead body. So while I was test-driving a possible romance with Mo Russert, Lynda had been mentally trying on the moniker Sister Lynda. I felt like a heel until I remembered that Lynda had been the one who wanted to break up. It didn't matter anyway. That was a long time ago—seven years in dog time!—and only our future mattered, not the past.

But Lynda wanted to explain.

"I don't know if you can understand this, but back then I didn't think we were going anywhere. And if you and I weren't meant to be, I didn't think there was any other man for me." *Well, sure, I can understand that.* "And I'd always been somewhat drawn to the religious life. When I met Polly at taekwondo class and I saw what a happy person she was, I started to think about it again. I went to a retreat with the Sisters of St. Augustine, talked with Polly about it, tried to get my head around it."

"And what did Polly say?" *I just want to know whether I should hate her or not.*

"She said I'd be a good fit for the community." I frowned. "But she also said religious life wasn't a place to hide and that I should work out my feelings for you first."

Whew. "I'm glad you took her advice."

"Well, it was good advice, wasn't it?"

I responded non-verbally.

George Apple was sitting in the parlor, waiting up for his wife, when I returned to Shamrocks & Ivy. With his feet up and his snowy hair disheveled, he somehow looked older. When he saw me, he picked up the remote and turned down the sound on the television.

"What's new, Sherlock?"

His child-like fascination with my investigative pursuits was kind of touching. I guessed this was the most exciting thing that had ever happened to him.

"Justin Bird turned himself in this morning," I reported.

"That's a relief! I feel safer knowing that he's in jail."

"He isn't. Not yet, anyway." I explained about Erica Slade and the likelihood that it would be a couple of days before Justin talked to Oscar.

"So where is he now?" George asked.

"I guess he's with his mother. From what I hear, it's not much of a home but it's the only one he's got."

"Bill Kirtland's sister came to pick up his stuff this afternoon."

Before I could ask George for details, the door opened behind me. I turned around. It took my brain about half a minute to process that it was Amy Quong coming through the doors. She'd let her hair down and donned a satiny dress the color of the emerald in Lynda's engagement ring.

"Good evening." She smiled, confirming my suspicion that she was pretty when she exercised her mouth muscles in the proper way. I also lowered my estimate of her age to late thirties, very early forties.

I stood up and mumbled some clumsy compliment about her dress.

"I've just come from the play and dinner at The Roundhouse before that." Ricoletti's only real competition for fine dining in Sussex County is a former railroad roundhouse converted to a restaurant back in the 1980s. "I found the play most enjoyable. Your Professor McCabe made a quite convincing Mycroft Holmes."

"Sally will be home soon," George said, standing up. "I'd better get her tea started. Care for a cup, Ms. Quong?"

"Not this late, thank you."

Engaged but not dead, I felt slightly awkward being left alone in the parlor with an attractive woman. Amy Quong gave no hint of any such awkwardness.

"Do you play chess?" she asked.

I followed her eyes and saw a board set up between two wingback chairs. It was a handsome Isle of Lewis chess set, the kind used in the first Harry Potter movie.

"A little," I said. I'd only been playing about five years. I knew I was in trouble when somebody asked on a chess website whether a person could ever be good at chess if he or she didn't start until age twenty-seven. The answer, basically, was that you could still have fun with the game. And I did.

"Let's play," she said, and sat. So did I.

And what game are we playing, Madame Quong? Maybe I'd seen too many flicks where a chess game is a metaphor or a turning point, but my discomfort at being alone with her didn't ease any.

She put a chess piece in each hand and asked me to pick. I drew black, meaning that she started the game. I'll give you the moves in case you play. If you don't play, there's no need to feel left out. I'll tell you all you really need to know. It started like this:

W: e4
B: e5
W: Nf3
B: Nf6

Those are rather standard opening moves. We each had advanced our King's pawn and then moved out the Knight. It's always good to move out your Knight and Bishop early.

"I understand you are getting married," she said as I waited for her next move.

I'm glad that's clear!

"Yeah—not long now."

"Congratulations. Have you thought of buying a home?"

Interesting question. "My fiancée and I haven't worked that out yet, but it's certainly a possibility."

W: Nxe5
B: Nex4

We each had moved our Knights again, capturing a pawn. Conventional wisdom is that you shouldn't touch the same piece more than once in the opening game. I suspected she wasn't a very good player, but I went along for the ride, mirroring her move.

As she bent over the board I caught a whiff of perfume. It was the delightful Cleopatra VII, Lynda's favorite. I also caught site of a lovely pair of half-moon earrings, silver embedded with diamonds.

"What beautiful earrings!"

"Thank you. It's the pair I thought I'd lost. They turned out to be in my jewelry box after all."

I'm glad that at least one mystery has been solved.

"I would really urge you to buy a home," my opponent said. "Prices are still low and mortgage rates are the lowest they've been in decades. I think you'll find that at Gamble Bank our rates are very competitive. And we can handle all your banking needs just like our competitors that are not locally based."

So that was her angle—a sales pitch for her bank. Dressed like one of Fu Manchu's wives she was still a banker. I felt so used. Then all of a sudden it clicked: One of Bill Kirtland's cases involved the search for a missing bank employee, an embezzler named Allison Lee. Lee could be an Asian name, couldn't it? What if Kirtland had found Allison Lee? What if I were playing chess with her right now?

W: Nxf7

Now I saw the trouble I was in. Ms. Quong, by moving her Knight yet again, was forcing me into a stupid move. Nobody moves the King in the opening game. But if my King didn't take her Knight, the Knight would take my Rook—a major piece. So I did.

B: Kxf7

"How did you happen to come here?" I asked.

"I needed a place to stay before I get possession of my home. One of my colleagues at the bank suggested this place. We hold the mortgage on it."

"Well, I hope they're not behind on payments." I smiled to show I was kidding, but Ms. Quong was all business.

"It would be highly inappropriate for me to comment on that," she said. I figured that meant she was there to measure the drapes for the foreclosure sale. "Check."

She had played:

W: Qh5+

With the Queen checking my King, I had to move the King out of her way. There were four options. I picked the worst.

B: Kg8

"Actually, I meant how did you come to Erin?"

"A headhunter called me about the position at Gamble and I was willing to relocate."

"Relocate from where?"

W: Qd5++

"Checkmate."

I stared at the board, looking for an out that wasn't there. She had beaten me in six moves. That squashed my suspicion that she wasn't a very good player. But I hadn't resolved all of my suspicions.

Ms. Quong stood up. "Thank you for the game, Mr. Cody. It was delightful. And do keep Gamble Bank in mind when you are ready to buy a home."

Chapter Twenty-Seven
Suspicions

I woke up Sunday to astonishing news: The Cain child had been recovered in Athens, safe and sound. Details were sketchy, but it turned out that he had been kidnapped. The parents initially hadn't told the police because of dire warnings about what would happen to the child if the kidnapping were reported. So the parents had suffered through the painful suspicion that they had harmed their child, and did so for their child's sake.

The kidnappers were a twenty-year-old man and his seventeen-year-old girlfriend. A keen-eyed clerk at a United Dairy Farmers convenience store had recognized the child from the Amber Alert when the three of them had stopped to buy diapers for the little boy.

With soaring faith in happy endings, I bounced downstairs to grab a cup of decaf before picking Lynda up for 9 A.M. Mass at St. Edward the Confessor Church. I found myself alone at the table with the Apples. Ms. Quong apparently was sleeping in, no doubt exhausted from her chess triumph of the night before.

"I think Professor McCabe is getting a little frustrated with Mr. Figg," Sally said.

What gave you your first clue—the shouting or the screaming?
"More drama before the drama?" I asked.

She nodded, sitting next to me conspiratorially. She was wearing an apron over her Pillsbury Doughboy shape even though she wasn't cooking yet.

"Friday it was changes in the script," she said. "Yesterday Mr. Figg was telling the professor how to stand."

"Well, he is the director. I guess a director is supposed to direct." *Although I'm not sure Mac would agree.*

I swallowed the last of my decaf and pedaled over to Lynda's apartment under cloudy skies, just ahead of a thunderstorm.

After Mass and the obligatory chat with Fr. Nguyen, we drove over to Mac's house for brunch. It rankled that I was paying for a bed and breakfast and not getting the breakfast, but Sunday brunch at the McCabes is an old habit. Also, the food is good now that Mac handles the Sunday cooking instead of my sister.

Lynda's parents had been invited to join us. "But they're sleeping in," Kate said.

I repressed a snicker.

"How are you and Lucia getting along?" I asked.

Kate is one of the kindest people I know, even when she is being a slightly bossy older sister. "Ms. Schiaparelli is certainly . . . vivacious and memorable," she said with the subtlety of the artist that she is. "But we haven't seen her all that much. She's been eating all her meals out for some reason."

I thought I knew the reason. Kate is no artist of the skillet and oven.

"Well, I've seen plenty of her," Lynda said glumly.

Brunch was the usual noisy affair with the three McCabe children present—Rebecca, almost thirteen (as she puts it); Amanda, ten; and Brian, just turned eight going on eighteen. After they cleared out, it was time to talk murder.

"Oscar called me late last night," Mac reported. "I suspect he was trying to catch me sleeping, but he was unsuccessful. He told me that there were two calls to Bill Kirtland's cell phone on the evening of the murder—one at 7:23 and one at 9:23. The caller is unknown, however, because the phone number—with a local area code, by the way—is that of an untraceable cell phone. It has probably been thrown away by now."

"What about photos?" Lynda asked. "Were there any of those on the phone?"

Mac shook his head. "There were no photos or video from Erin on Kirtland's cell phone, and nothing that was helpful. Candidly, I am not surprised. The killer would be dull indeed not to destroy that phone if there were any chance it held incriminating evidence."

"Then why did you tell Oscar to look for a picture?" I said.

"Because many, perhaps most, killers are dull indeed."

"So it looks like he was lured to his death by those phone calls." I realize that the phrase "lured to his death" is a cliché, but I don't edit myself very well in conversation. I thought about Miles Archer in _The Maltese Falcon_ being shot in an alley and his partner, Sam Spade, figuring out that he was too good a detective to turn his back on a stranger. "It had to be somebody he knew," I said.

"It would seem so," Mac conceded. "And yet he knew no one in Erin except Polly, unless we count his good friend Justin Bird. Most intriguing! I have an additional piece of information from Oscar: Mary Rose Kirtland said her brother's Walther wasn't among his effects."

"You mean he might have been shot with his own gun?" Kate asked.

Noting the incredulous look on her face, Mac said, "It does seem difficult to believe, does it not, that a private investigator, a veteran of Army counterintelligence, would have permitted that to happen? And I find it particularly hard to credit that Justin Bird, who was so incompetent at following Kirtland in the car, would be able to secure his gun and use it to shoot him from behind. That would be an untenable theory even without the logistics of Justin having to leave the theater from the back or side, where Kirtland would see his approach."

Lynda's gold-flecked brown eyes glinted with the fire of a new-born idea. "How do we even know he brought the gun with him? Maybe he left it at home and somebody else stole it to use on him—his sister! She's his sole survivor with three children to support and a husband who's negligent with his child support payments."

Hey, that's good! Wish I'd thought of it!

"But from what Mac said, she and her brother were close," Kate pointed out.

"And how do we know that?" Lynda shot back. "Only because Mary Rose Kirtland said so! She could have been feeding you and Oscar a line."

Just for fun I shook my head and adopted an expression of sadness. "So young and yet so cynical you are, Lynda." Moving quickly to exit the doghouse before the door slammed shut, I added, "You're right, of course. But we could ask Polly. She might be able to tell us how the Kirtlands got along."

"Or at least what their relationship was when she and Bill were dating," Lynda said. "That could have changed in the years since." She was already texting, presumably to Polly, as she spoke. I decided this was the time to share my own brainstorm.

"I played chess with one of my housemates last night, Amy Quong," I said.

Mac raised an eyebrow. I usually don't know what he means by that, and sometimes I think he doesn't know either. Lynda looked up from her texting and regarded me as if to say, *"Where does that fit in?"* But what she actually said was, "That must have been pretty late."

Not really. I'd pedaled back to the Shamrocks & Ivy from Lynda's place about ten o'clock.

"The game didn't last long," I said.

"How badly did she beat you?" Mac asked.

"Brutal" would be a kind word for it. "That's irrelevant, Mac. What's important is that Amy Quong is a very shrewd

cookie, and a banker at Gamble. One of Kirtland's open cases was a missing woman who'd embezzled from a bank. And that woman's last name is Lee, which could be Asian, which Ms. Quong definitely is. I think we should at least see what we can find out about this Allison Lee."

"Being a good chess player is 'always the mark of a scheming mind,' according to Sherlock Holmes," Mac said. "Certainly your suspicions are worth pursuing. We must ask Oscar to find out more about this missing bank embezzler." He glanced at his Sherlock Holmes watch and stood up. "I had best be on my way."

It was almost noon and the Sunday matinee of *1895* started at 2 P.M.

"Have fun with Figg," I said insincerely. That sounded like the title of a kid's book: *Fun with Figg!* "Hey, whatever came of your mutterings that he was up to something at the library?"

"He was," Mac said darkly. "Strangely, my juvenile taunt about the location of Sherlock Holmes was not misdirected. He actually was looking for Holmes books." My face must have registered complete dismay. I assumed that all Sherlockians had hundreds of books about their hero. Mac did. He hastened to explain:

"Lafcadio is something of an expert on theatrical and film adaptations of the Holmes adventures—at least he thinks he is—but he is no scholar of the Canon. Feeling that our staging of the play was somewhat amiss, he sought out Arthur Twidle's original *Strand* magazine illustrations of 'The Adventure of the Bruce-Partington Plans' for inspiration. He found them in Les Klinger's *New Annotated Sherlock Holmes* and decided we needed to emulate those drawings."

"Word on the street is that you didn't react well," I said, recalling Sally Apple's account of his frustration.

"This isn't his favorite subject," my sister inserted helpfully as she started to clear the table.

"To be candid," Mac said, "I felt hoist on my own petard. I could scarcely complain about Lafcadio attempting to make our little drama more authentic, could I?"

"Why did he go to the public library instead of the Woollcott Chalmers Collection at St. Benignus?" Kate wondered. "The Collection is much more comprehensive if you're looking for art of Sherlock Holmes."

Mac smiled broadly. "I have a strong suspicion that my old friend was afraid he might encounter me on the St. Benignus campus, which he would find embarrassing."

Oh, the delicious irony!

Lynda looked up from her smart phone. "Polly says that Bill Kirtland talked about his sister and her kids a lot, even in the brief time he was here. He used to be close to her, and Polly has no reason to think he wasn't still." She shrugged. "Oh, well, my idea would have worked for Columbo."

Mac's cell phone rang, if you can call *Ride of the Valkyries* a ring.

"Oh, hello, Oscar, we were just talking about the case. What! How badly? What is his condition? When did this happen? Were there any witnesses? I see. Thank you for calling. Please keep me posted."

He disconnected. "Justin Bird was run down by a hit-and-run driver this morning. He is in a coma at St. Hildegard Hospital and the prognosis for his survival is guarded."

Chapter Twenty-Eight
Close to Home

"Good morning, Popcorn," I said as I breezed past her on my way into my office in Carey Hall on Monday morning.

"The face is familiar but I forget the name," my administrative assistant replied.

Her sarcasm was not undeserved, considering how little time I'd spent in the office the last few days of the previous week.

She followed me and stood in my doorway as I sat down at my desk.

"Did Col. Teal catch up to you on Friday?"

"We spent most of the day together." *Hey, wait a minute.* "What do you mean 'catch up' with me?"

"He came here looking for you. I told him you'd be over at Daniel's for lunch."

"Oh, yeah, sure."

So Jake didn't just happen to come into Daniel's while I was having lunch. That being the case, he also probably didn't just happen to spend the day with me showing Bill Kirtland's picture all over town. *What the hell did that mean?* The question was playing at the back of my mind the entire ten minutes or so it took Popcorn to fill me in on everything she'd neglected to tell me during our frequent telephone contacts on Friday. There wasn't much. Spring semester exams had started and everybody was behaving, including Ralph Pendergast. Not a single athlete—or professor, for that matter—had been arrested.

"The first responses to our RFPs from web designers have started coming in," Popcorn said. "Four arrived in Friday's mail."

"Are any of them worth an interview?"

"One definite and one maybe."

The Request for Proposals had gone out a couple of weeks before when I'd convinced Ralph that it was time to update our aging website, which had first appeared in its current iteration way back before the dawn of the Blogosphere. There had been a few cosmetic changes in the site over the years, but it wasn't nearly interactive enough. A committee would interview representatives of the final four candidates and make a choice over the summer. If it were up to me, I would have replaced the whole committee—including me—with Popcorn, but it wasn't up to me.

After she left my office, I spent about thirty seconds wondering whether I should be glad or worried that Popcorn ran our little operation flawlessly without me and was more than willing to cover for my absences in return for the inside story about the latest McCabe escapade.

Half a minute was all I could devote to that question before my mind focused again on the puzzling matter of Jake Teal. Why did he spend all that time with me as I pursued a task that was certainly boring and most likely to be fruitless? As I thought about Bill Kirtland, I remembered the cases his sister said he's been working on. One of them involved the military, something about corruption on a contract. A lot of money could be at stake in something like that . . . and a career, too. That added up to a very solid murder motive for whomever Kirtland was investigating.

Before I knew it I was wondering what kind of gun Jake Teal carried, that gun he was so eager to point at Justin Bird. I'd seen it, but I don't know a .22 from a .45.

DA-da-da-da—DA-da-da! The Indiana Jones ring-tone cut through my suspicious musings. It was Mac. We hadn't spoken since he went off to the play, leaving me and my dear fiancée to go tell Triple M what had happened to Justin. The distraught sister immediately saw the hit-and-run as evidence that there was a killer out there who, for some inscrutable reason, wanted to get rid of Justin as well as Bill Kirtland. I had my doubts. Accidents do happen, and most hit-and-run cases are accidents.

"Good morning, Jefferson! I hope I am not interrupting anything important." Without waiting to find out whether he was, Mac went on: "I am pleased to report that our investigation is moving forward on several fronts."

"That's nice, but what do you hear about Justin?" Getting meaningful patient information out of hospitals these days is like trying to get the formula for Coca-Cola.

"According to Oscar, his condition has not changed. Oscar also told me that a witness identified the offending vehicle as a silver-gray Honda Accord."

"That's a break!" So it wasn't Jake Teal's car.

"Yes and no. Gibbons found a car matching that description abandoned two blocks from Justin's mother's house, where he was hit. It had been stolen, so that is likely to be unhelpful. In the course of our conversation, I asked Oscar to get us additional information and a photo of the missing Allison Lee."

Oh, yeah. Allison Lee. My suspicious mind had been running along another track this morning. I told Mac about Jake Teal's deception.

"Most intriguing," he commented. "I wish I were going to be there to confront him with the truth."

"You are." I wasn't about to do that alone. I felt that I'd developed a certain rapport with Jake, but that might quickly be flushed down the toilet when I asked him why he'd lied to me, at least by implication.

So Mac agreed to help me through this. We decided together to ask Jake to come over to my office around ten o'clock. We'd picked my office because it would be handy to have Popcorn in the next office if I needed to have her repeat what she'd told me.

I texted Lynda, got Jake's phone number from her, and called him. "I've got some new questions to pursue on this Kirtland murder and I was hoping you could help me," I said with total honesty.

"Happy to help if I can, son! It's not like I'm overly busy these days. I was just sitting here alone on your couch reading one of Mac's books."

Well, if you're on my couch, I'm glad you're alone.

Jake was available at the chosen time and agreed to meet me in the office. He didn't have to ask where it was, of course, since he'd been there before. And I didn't tell him that Mac was part of the package.

Mac arrived about ten minutes before the appointed hour, bringing news.

"Mary Rose Kirtland just called me," he said, squeezing into one of the two chairs in front of my desk. "She called the client in the fiancé investigation case and secured his permission to give us his contact information. His name is Paul Woodford and he lives a little north of Louisville. I will telephone him as soon as we are finished with Col. Teal. If he is willing to talk to us, we could be at his doorstep two hours after that."

"That's with you driving at your usual unlawful, breakneck speed," I said. "Can't we just call him on the phone?"

"We may have to, if he refuses to see us. But personal interviews are always better. Body language seldom lies."

"You're expecting Kirtland's client to lie?" Mac raised an eyebrow. "I always do, old boy."

"Morning, Jeff." Jake Teal strode into the room like a handsome retired Army officer nattily dressed in pressed khakis and a button-down shirt. *Oh, yeah, I guess he would.* "Hi, Mac. Surprised to see you here." Sometimes Jake sounded more southern than other times, and that was one of them.

Mac nodded at Jake while I said, "Have a seat."

"I thought you wanted me to go sleuthing with you, like Friday."

"You can help me right here, if you'd be so kind."

"Sure, whatever I can do."

Once my future father-in-law had made himself at home, I looked him straight in his gray eyes and told myself I wasn't nervous. *Like hell I'm not. And I hope Mac is watching your trigger finger.*

"What you can do, Jake, is tell us the truth," I said.

He looked at Mac, who looked about as expressive as a president on Mt. Rushmore, then back at me. "Say what?"

"It was no coincidence that you and I wound up at Daniel's Apothecary together on Friday—Popcorn told you where I was. You were looking for me. What was that all about?"

He gave an *aw shucks, you caught me* kind of grin. "Oh, that. I was just being the worried father of the bride, that's all. Look, my daughter's marrying a guy I'd never met until a few days ago. I wanted to spend a little time with you, size you up. When you weren't in your office, I figured maybe that was for the best—that you'd be less defensive, less on your guard if I ran into you by accident. Okay, maybe I'm an overly protective father. So shoot me."

Funny you should put it that way, Jake.

"What kind of gun is that you're packing?" I asked.

He looked down, as if surprised to find it there. "My old service weapon, a 9mm Parabellum. Why?"

So not a Walter PPK/S .380.

Ignoring his question, Mac said, "I take it that you didn't know Bill Kirtland."

Jake knit his brows together, as if puzzled. "No, of course not. I never heard of him until he was killed."

"You were both in the Army at the same time," I pointed out.

"Are you crazy?" His daughter had asked me a similar question on more than one occasion. "So were more than half a million other soldiers."

"We have learned that Bill Kirtland was working on some kind of corruption investigation involving military contracts," Mac said.

Jake let it lay there.

"I guess you're going to say you never had anything to do with military contracts," I said finally.

"Me? Of course I didn't—other than maybe reporting on them. I was an FA46. That's public affairs, which includes journalism. I know you said Lynda didn't tell you what I did, but I assumed you'd know at least that much. My last assignment was mostly dealing with the national news media at the Pentagon. I guess you could say we're kind of in the same business, Jeff."

I felt as though I was looking at the world through a kaleidoscope and somebody had just turned the tube. Somehow this was more disorienting than finding out that Triple M had been in counterintelligence. I never would have imagined Jake Teal for a wordsmith. But did it really change anything? I'd have to think that through. His story of why he'd attached himself to me on Friday seemed plausible enough. I wondered what Mac thought of it.

"Kind of," I muttered. "We'll have to talk shop, compare notes. I'm sure you've had some interesting experiences."

"That I have."

For now, though, the wind had been taken out of my sails. Mac didn't have any more questions either.

"Thank you for suffering through our little inquisition," Mac said. "With your background I am sure you understand the value of sometimes asking questions to which one thinks one knows the answer."

Jake nodded almost as if he believed that. He stood up. "I guess I'll go, then. By the way, Mac, in case you didn't notice,

I finally got to your play yesterday afternoon. That was good stuff."

"You can thank my source material. I just translated it to the stage." *With a little help from Lafcadio Figg.*

"I liked the twist in the solution. After all that talk of spies, the killer turned out to be somebody close to home."

He shook our hands and left. But something he'd said stayed behind with me—"close to home." We'd already speculated that the killer would most easily be somebody that Kirtland knew, and we'd tried on his sister for size. But what about somebody who was close to home in the sense of living in Erin?

The idea that Triple M, my cheerful and optimistic friend, would deliberately hurt anybody was just ridiculous, of course. I couldn't even say it out loud to Mac. But I could think it. While Mac was calling Paul Woodford in Kentucky to see if we could come and talk to him about Bill Kirtland's investigation of his daughter's fiancé, I let the idea play out in my head.

Was there a motive? Maybe Kirtland did still have romantic feelings and he pressed them hard. *She shot him in the back of the head in self-defense? No, that wouldn't work.* Maybe she feared scandal. What was so scandalous about the fact that they'd dated, no matter how you define dating? The past is past—unless there was something else we didn't know.

One thing for sure was that Triple M knew how to shoot a gun. She would have learned that in the Army.

Chapter Twenty-Nine
Case Closed

Ten minutes later, Triple M wasn't even on my mind any more. We were in Mac's vintage red Chevy headed toward the Louisville area. After Paul Woodford had finally agreed to talk to us—despite some initial resistance—I'd told Popcorn that we were heading out to an early lunch and I might be late.

"See you tomorrow, Boss."

"Don't worry, I'll check in before that."

"I wasn't worried."

While Mac drove, I called Lynda.

"Why the hell didn't you tell me that your father was in journalism and public affairs for the Army?"

"Good morning to you, too, sweetheart," she said sweetly. "Didn't you get enough sleep? You seem a little cranky."

"I thought he was, like, Special Forces or something, the way he always carries a gun."

"A lot of people carry guns," she huffed, "even Mac!" Lynda is so cute when she huffs. "I'm sorry that Daddy disappointed you."

"I'm not disappointed." *Relieved would be a better word.* "It's just that he comes across as such a tough guy."

"Oh, he is. Who says a journalist can't be a tough guy—especially when you're helping tell the story of a war? During the Gulf War in '91 he had to shoot his way out of an ambush. Daddy was the only survivor. He never told me, though, not even when I asked him about the medal. One of his old buddies did."

I took a breath to steady myself. "You ought to be proud of that."

"Oh, I am."

"But why didn't you tell me your father was a communications guy? Didn't you know I'd be interested?"

She sighed. "Maybe it was habit. When I first got into journalism, Daddy was the editor of *Stars & Stripes Europe*. I never wanted anybody to know I was in the same field as my father. I was afraid people would think that's why I chose journalism, like it wasn't totally and completely my own idea. And now it's even worse that I'm marrying a guy who basically does the same thing Daddy did at the end of his Army career. That has Electra Complex written all over it."

"A *wonderful* guy," I commented, not sure what Carmen Electra had to do with this (just kidding). "You should have said, 'Now that I'm marrying a *wonderful* guy, etc.'"

"Correction noted and accepted. And I apologize. I'll try to make it up to you over the next sixty years. Meanwhile, my mother has a new idea. She says she should be the one to give me away."

When I write a book about this, it will be filed with the fiction.

Paul Woodford, a builder who dabbled in local politics, had asked Mac to meet him at the county building where he had his office as judge executive, the top elected official of the county. It was a solid, grim old building on the outside that somebody had cheered up on the inside with bright lights and colorful carpeting.

Woodford was a big guy in his late-fifties with a flop-over-the-belt belly, thinning sandy hair, and a red face. The collar of his white shirt was open at his bovine neck and the knot on his tie was pulled down. I wouldn't have wanted to be his life insurance agent.

"Make yourself at home," he said cordially, waving in the direction of four chairs at a side table in his spacious quarters. "Coffee?"

We accepted the seats, begged off on the java. Woodford joined us at the round table.

"Like I told you on the phone, it's all over," he said. "That's why I tried to talk you fellas out of coming all this way. The case is closed, I guess you could say. Kirtland already turned in his report on Wednesday. He wasn't working for me anymore, the poor bastard. Pardon my French."

"May we ask the results of his investigation?" Mac asked.

"Sure. It doesn't matter now. But I guess I'd better background you a little on that first." He got up and poured himself a cup of coffee from a pot on a credenza. He held up the pot. "You're sure?" We were sure.

"I'm a wealthy man," he said as he settled back down. "No, scratch that. I'm rich. When my daughter gets engaged about a month ago to some guy still in college at UK from a family I never heard of, my little antennae go up, see?" He made little antennae over his head with his fingers. "I'm thinking 'gold-digger' and 'gigolo.' So I start asking around the court house for the name of somebody who can ask a few questions for me, quiet-like. Somebody gave me the name of this Kirtland."

"Do you remember who?" Mac asked.

"No. Does that matter?"

"I doubt it. What did Kirtland turn up?"

He chuckled ruefully. "This kid, Dalton Purvis is his name, should run for public office. He would drive the background-checkers nuts trying to find dirt. He raised a prize-winning cow in 4-H, made Eagle Scout, even saved a little girl from drowning one summer when he worked as a life-guard. Oh, and his grade point average is 4.0. He's a graduating senior, took his final exams on May 4."

"What's his major?" I asked.

Mac looked at me like *what the hell?* But I was curious, and I hadn't asked Woodford a question yet.

"Pre-law."

"Well, you must be a happy guy," I said, all smiles despite the fact that this drive had been a complete waste of time. "Your future son-in-law is already a saint and he's going to be a lawyer. Sit back and enjoy the wedding."

Woodford shook his head mournfully, looking like a basset hound. "Too late for that. Somehow Tiffany got wind that I'd hired a private investigator to look into her stud muffin. Maybe her mother let it slip, I don't know. Anyway, Tiffany eloped over the weekend. She sent her mother a text from Reno. Talk about backfiring! And all I was trying to do is protect my little girl."

I stifled my envy at the elopement and hauled out the sympathy. "Gee, that's a shame for you. I'm sure you would have liked to walk her down the aisle. Maybe you could still have a party."

"I hope so, fella. I already put down a deposit on the hall."

"Obviously, Dalton Purvis has no motive and—on the face of it—a solid alibi in Reno," Mac was saying as we walked out of the county building. If there was a "but" coming, I never heard it because the *Ride of the Valkyries* interrupted. Mac whipped out his cell phone.

"Oh, hello, Oscar."

I won't bother you with Mac's side of the conversation, which ranged in tone from "I see" to "hmmph!" to "Indeed, this changes everything."

As we settled into Mac's car for the return trip home, Mac gave me the low down.

"Oscar has a photo of Allison Lee in hand and she is African American, not Asian," he said.

"Well, that's that." At least it was definitive, although I still didn't trust somebody who beat me at chess that quickly.

"Oscar had much bigger news than that, however," Mac went on. "Have you been following the case of young Bart Cain? He was an eighteen-month-old child who went missing in Athens earlier this week and it turned out to be a kidnapping."

"Yeah, I've been catching snatches of the saga for days on television and in the newspaper. It had a happy ending for a change. So?"

"So the police in Athens have informed Oscar that the boy's grandfather paid the ransom and hired someone to deliver it."

"And what's that got to do with us?"

"The person he hired was Bill Kirtland. Kirtland was supposed to deliver the money and pick up the child. According to the kidnappers, he never showed up."

Chapter Thirty
Old Ben

All of sudden I had a vision in my mind of that first night at Shamrocks & Ivy. The other car parked there was a Ford Fusion with a child's car seat in the back. I'd later learned that was Kirtland's car, but the anomaly of the car seat just hadn't registered.

"Oscar doesn't believe the kidnappers' story," Mac went on. "He thinks Kirtland was lured out of the theater by the kidnappers, killed so he could never identify them, and the ransom money taken. Quote: 'After all your amateur theories, it was just a very simple case of a kidnapping gone sour. I'll apologize to Justin if he ever comes out of the coma.' That's how Oscar sees it."

"How do you see it?"

"I predict that by tomorrow even Oscar will have buyer's remorse over that theory. It has more holes than a sieve. The kidnappers were a couple of lost souls, not master criminals. How would they know Kirtland was in Erin? How would they manage to shoot him with his own gun? Why would they kill him when they got what they wanted? What did they intend to do with the child—if they weren't going to give him back, why not kill him immediately? Would they really have the presence of mind to acquire a throwaway cell phone with a local number to call Kirtland? Where is the ransom money now? I may have more questions later, but those occur to me immediately."

"Maybe we shouldn't look a gift horse's ass in the mouth," I said. "We got involved in this mess to help Justin. Right now it looks like the only help he needs is going to come from doctors. Isn't our job finished?"

Mac regarded me as though I were an alien species. "Someone killed Bill Kirtland. I believe that same someone tried to kill Justin Bird with a stolen car. Surely you do not propose that we simply let that person get away with it and go about our business?"

Actually, that's just what I had in mind. I have a wedding to worry about.

"No, of course not," I muttered. Mac picked up his cell phone. "What are you doing?"

"Since Providence has brought us here to the Louisville area, it would be wasteful indeed not to take advantage of our location by talking with Ben Cain. He knows more than anyone alive about Bill Kirtland's connection to the kidnapping, and perhaps about his trip to Erin as well."

Forget about that whole six degrees of separation thing when it comes to Sebastian McCabe. He can connect himself to anyone on the planet with two or three phone calls. In this case it took three, starting with a member of the Sherlock Holmes group in Louisville. Within ten minutes he was talking to Ben Cain himself. Cain suggested that we meet for a drink in the Lobby Bar at the Brown Hotel in downtown Louisville.

On the way over, Mac couldn't resist reminding me of a minor issue on which he'd been right.

"It seems that there was indeed a reason, even if perhaps only subconscious, why Kirtland picked *Hocus-Pocus* out of all my books to reread," he said. "The plot, as you will recall, involved a kidnapping."

Big deal. Don't dislocate your arm patting yourself on the back. I studied the GPS on my iPhone.

The Brown is a legendary hotel in the grand manner at the corner of Fourth and Broadway in downtown Louisville, built in 1923. The open-faced turkey and bacon sandwich called the Hot Brown was invented there. I'd heard of it, but never been there. When we walked into the two-story marble and mahogany lobby, I wasn't sure whether I'd stepped into another era or just a level of living above my pay grade.

"I hope he's buying," I said to Mac *sotto voce*. "I'm not sure I could afford a Diet Coke here."

Ben Cain wasn't holding up a sign, like people in airports looking for somebody, but he didn't need to. Sitting by himself at a small, square table between the ornate wood bar and a highly polished baby grand piano, he looked like a man waiting for somebody. An amber liquid in a rocks glass with no ice sat in front of him. He was a handsome, distinguished man in his eighties, wearing a three-piece suit about the same shade of gray as his hair. I'd been expecting somebody a few decades younger if his grandson was only eighteen months old. When he saw us, he stood up with the aid of a cane that had the head of a dog carved in wood on the top. He was about half a foot shorter than me.

"Mr. McCabe and Mr. Cody?" he asked. We admitted it. "My old friend Father Joe speaks very highly of both of you. Yes, I made a few calls to check you out, even though you are a friend of a friend. Have a seat." We did. "Have some peanuts or pretzels. How about a drink? You'll never guess what I'm having."

"Tea?" I guessed. It was a test. I wanted to see if he had a sense of humor.

He chuckled. "Kentucky tea, I suppose you could call it. I always drink plain Old Ben. We make lots of different products now, small batch and single barrel and whatnot, and it's all good. But I'll stick by Old Ben, the bourbon my granddaddy's granddaddy made." He gave a little salute with his glass and took a healthy sip. Apparently 3 P.M. is cocktail hour in Louisville. "Family is very important to me, gentlemen."

A waiter with curly black hair and a light blue tie approached, but I waved him off.

"I can understand that, sir," Mac said. "You must have been very shocked when you learned that your grandson had been kidnapped."

Ben Cain looked at us. "Do you have children?"

"I have three," Mac said.

"I have hopes," I said. "I'm getting married in twelve days." *Twelve days—holy shit!*

"Congratulations, young man. I didn't marry until I was fifty-five, myself, but my wife is quite a bit younger and we were able to have five children. Let me tell you, it's not easy having children when you're older, but you appreciate them more. Bart is our first grandson. When his daddy called me and told me that he'd been taken"—he gulped more of the family bourbon—"I was just shaken, scared shitless. Anybody who has a little money is always afraid of something like that, but still, I never really thought . . ."

He stared ahead.

"I gather the kidnappers knew that Bart's grandfather was a man of means," Mac said.

"That would be a safe assumption. They asked for a lot more money than my professor son could put his hands on in a hurry."

"And how much was that?"

I had this vision of Dr. Evil in *Austin Powers* saying "One *mil*lion dollars!" But apparently the kidnappers had never seen that classic film.

"Two hundred and fifty thousand," Cain said. "Kind of insulting, isn't it? I mean, it would be a lot for my son but not for me. Maybe they figured it would be easier for me to put up such a small amount, or that I would be more likely to pay it without a fuss." He finished off the bourbon. "I'll tell you a secret: Whatever they wanted, I would have given it to them if I had it. Listen, J. Paul Getty was the richest man in the world when his grandson was kidnapped in the 1970s. Getty refused to pay the ransom, so they cut off the kid's ear—a sixteen-year-old kid. Then the old man paid." Cain shook his head. "Can you believe that? I couldn't let them hurt Bart, no way. That's why I followed their instructions to the letter."

"And one of their instructions was to not go to the police," I recalled.

"That's right. I was to have the money in Athens on Friday—they gave me a couple of days to get the cash together. They were going to call me to tell me exactly when and where to make the exchange, the money for Bart. I could designate someone else to bring the money, but the police were not to know or we would never see Bart again. I couldn't take a chance that they were bluffing. I know enough about the history of kidnapping to know that Bart's chances weren't good even if they got the money. Kidnappers are rotten, murderous people, even though this pair sounded like a couple of kids. That's why I wanted somebody who could handle himself to take care of this for me."

"How did you settle on Bill Kirtland?" Mac asked.

Cain smiled. "I have friends. I called around. I needed somebody who was discreet and absolutely reliable because I was entrusting him with a lot more than two hundred and fifty thousand dollars—my grandson's life depended on him. A couple of people I trust recommended Kirtland. And I was impressed by his military background."

"If he was supposed to deliver the money to Athens, what was he doing in Erin?"

"It was part of our plan to shake off anybody who might be trying to follow him. He looked at a map and decided that Erin would be a good place to spend the night because he had a friend in town—that would give him a plausible reason for being there."

"I don't get that," I said. "Who were you afraid might be following him?"

"The police." Cain motioned to the waiter, who nodded. Another Old Ben, coming up. "I was afraid my son would crack under the pressure and tell them what had happened. Of course, I always planned that once we had Bart back I would make sure those scoundrels were caught and punished to the fullest extent of the law."

"A young man named Justin Bird followed Kirtland in Erin for dubious reasons that I need not get into now," Mac said. "Kirtland apparently thought he was one of the kidnappers. How was the money to be delivered?"

"A quarter of a million in small bills doesn't fit in a briefcase, so I put it in an old suitcase of mine—Big Blue, I call it. Kirtland was to drive to Athens and await further instructions on Friday morning. I'd given the kidnappers his cell phone number. You can imagine that I was terrified when I didn't hear anything back from him by late Friday night.

"Finally, early Saturday morning, the kidnappers called and said they hadn't been able to reach Kirtland. I didn't know about his murder, so I had no idea what was going on. The kidnappers accused me of jerking them around. They told me they'd kill Bart if I didn't deliver the money by Saturday night. I said I'd already given the money to Kirtland and I couldn't get together another quarter of a million that fast. I'm not sure they believed me, but they gave me until Monday. I don't think they wanted to end this thing without getting the money.

"At this point my son and I, not knowing whether Kirtland had skipped with the money or what, agreed that we'd better contact the authorities. They put out the story about Bart's parents being under suspicion so the kidnappers wouldn't suspect that we'd brought the police into the case. You know what happened then: Even with the police involved, it was just Providence that on Sunday Bart was spotted and the kidnappers taken."

"The money was not recovered, however," Mac noted.

The waiter brought old Ben another Old Ben. He saluted us with it and took a sip.

"Money is only money, gentleman," he said. "I can always get more of that. But don't get me wrong. I'd like to have the cash back. If you find it, I'll give you twenty percent. How's that for a finder's fee?"

"Very generous," I said. *Invested prudently in a well-balanced portfolio of stock and bond index funds, fifty thousand dollars could produce an annual return of* . . .

Mac stood up. "I cannot at the moment think of anything else. Can you, Jefferson?"

I couldn't, but Cain gave us each one of his cards with the company logo in case we thought of anything later. I looked at it for a moment, thinking what a legend he was in the bourbon industry.

"Can I have your autograph?" I asked. "My fianceé would love it."

Chapter Thirty-One
The Sleeper Awakes

"His autograph? My goodness, Jefferson!"

"I didn't ask for it on a bottle of bourbon," I protested. "That was his idea. Lynda will be thrilled, even though it's not her favorite brand. This is like a get-of-the-doghouse free card, if I ever need it."

We were in the big red McCabemobile, heading back to Erin. I had the bottle in my hand.

"What do you think happened to the money?" I asked.

"Until a better theory presents itself, I think it is safe to assume that the killer took the ransom money as well as Bill Kirtland's life. Even Oscar thinks that, although he casts the kidnappers in the unlikely roll of killers."

Mac's phone rang, or squawked, or whatever you call it when you hear *Ride of the Valkyries* coming out of a man's breast pocket. Ignoring the dirty look I give him whenever he talks on the phone while driving—especially when he's barreling up I-71 at seventy-five miles an hour with me in the death seat—he answered.

"Yes? Hello, Oscar. That is good news—good news indeed on many levels. Thank you for thinking of me. Oh? Did he see anything? That is unfortunate, albeit unsurprising. No, I do not suppose he needs Erica Slade's services any longer. Good-bye."

He disconnected.

"Justin?" I said.

Mac nodded. "He awoke from the coma this afternoon well enough for a visit from the police. At this point Oscar has no interest in him as a suspect, but he did ask him about the auto that hit him. Justin was able to describe the stolen vehicle, but not the driver."

"So again Justin doesn't know anything." I thought I was stating the obvious with this little dig, but not as far as Mac was concerned.

"On the contrary," he said. "Someone stole an auto and used it to try to kill Justin for a reason. I strongly suspect that Justin knows something. He just doesn't know that he knows it."

I hate it when he's being enigmatic.

"Well, if he doesn't know that he knows it," I said, "it's just the same as not knowing it, because we'll never know whatever it is that he knows but doesn't know that he knows."

Just don't make me say that again, because I couldn't.

"No, it is not quite the same, Jefferson. If Justin saw something that could implicate the killer, but it did not register as being important, he may have scarcely noticed with his conscious mind. It is still resident in his subconscious, however, just   waiting   to   be   coaxed   out."

"You mean by hypnosis?"

"Precisely, old boy!"

"Where are we going to get a hypnotist?"

"*I* am a hypnotist." Mac sounded offended, as if I was supposed to remember that. "It was part of my stock in trade when I was a magician in Europe. I once hypnotized the deputy prime minister of Italy and had him crow like a rooster."

I was unimpressed. "That can't have been very hard. He was a politician, so it came naturally. And that was—what? About twenty years ago?"

"One does not lose the skill, especially when one uses it from time to time in other contexts which it would not be prudent for me to discuss." A smile played on his lips. I'm glad I don't play cards with him.

It seemed to me that Mac was making two leaps of faith in one. He was assuming both that Justin had seen something, and that he could pull it out of him. No one has ever accused Sebastian McCabe of lacking self-confidence.

"So what's your plan?"

"The plan is simplicity itself. We should be able to reach the hospital before closing hours. With Justin's permission, I will hypnotize him, take him back to the night of the murder, and see what he saw."

"Text me with the results," I said.

He took his eyes off the road—always a bad move—and raised an eyebrow.

"I want you to drop me off at my office so I can put in a guest appearance," I explained. "I've had several e-mails that need attention in ways that can't be handled on the road." This was true, by the way. "Then I'm going to meet Lynda after her taekwondo class and give her this." I held up the autographed bottle of Old Ben. Before he could object, I added: "You won't be without an audience. Call Johanna Rawls. I promised to keep her in the loop. If this works out, she'll get the sexiest story of her young career."

"Yes, of course." Although he didn't take his hands off the wheel, in my mind's eye Mac was thoughtfully stroking the beard that wasn't there anymore.

And that's how it came about that I missed one of the best stunts of Mac's life and almost got myself and two other people killed in the process.

Since I wasn't present for Mac's "you are getting sleepy" routine, you'll have to read about it—as I did—in Johanna's story that ran the next day. It probably would have led the front page of *The Erin Observer & News-Ledger* if my near-death experience and the capture of the killer hadn't reduced it to a long feature-style sidebar.

Chapter Thirty-Two
"Your Eyelids Are Getting Heavy"

Excerpt from a story in The Erin Observer & News-Ledger, *May 15, 2012:*

HYPOTIC WITNESS
Former Suspect
Gives Information
While in Trance

(Editor's note:* Erin Observer & News Ledger reporter Johanna Rawls was present when Sebastian McCabe interviewed a key witness in the murder of William Kirtland. This is her exclusive eye-witness account.)

By Johanna Rawls
Staff Reporter

For three days high school dropout Justin Bird was a "person of interest" in the murder of private investigator William Kirtland, 36.

On Monday he became a key witness in the case.

The dramatic turn of events involved an interview while under hypnosis conducted at St. Hildegard of Bingen Hospital, where Bird is still recuperating from being hit by a car on Sunday.

Bird, 24, lay in a coma for more than twenty-four hours. When he awoke, Erin Police Chief Oscar Hummel rushed to St. Hildegard to interview him.

"He was no longer a person of interest in the murder because other suspects had emerged," said Hummel, referring to Aaron Saylor, 20, and Jennifer Cordes, 17. They were arrested earlier Monday in Athens, Ohio, where they live, in conjunction with a child kidnapping case in which Kirtland was retained by the victim's family. "But I wanted to see if he knew who tried to run him down. He didn't."

But Sebastian McCabe, the well-known mystery writer and amateur sleuth, had other questions for the hit-and-run victim.

"It was perfectly obvious from the first that the automobile assault on Justin was no accident but a murder attempt," said McCabe, who is also the Lorenzo Smythe Professor of English Literature and head of the popular culture program at St. Benignus College. "The auto was stolen and abandoned a short distance away after the driver left Justin for dead.

"I became convinced that Justin knew something about the murder, perhaps subconsciously, that made it imperative for the murderer to eliminate him. I resolved to learn what that was."

He arrived at the hospital to find Bird, a young man with a troubled past, weak but alert.

"Congratulations, Justin!" McCabe said.

"What for?" Bird replied. "I got hit by a car and they tell me I was in a coma."

"Ah, but you woke up. And as an added bonus, you are no longer a suspect in Bill Kirtland's murder. I wish to speak with you about what you saw backstage the night of the killing."

Bird shook his shaved head. "I already told you, Professor, I didn't see nothing."

"You know that cannot be true, Justin. You saw many things. You meant to say that you saw nothing important, and I am sure you believe that. I believe differently, however."

McCabe went on to explain that he, Bird, may have seen something revealing about the killer without consciously noticing it at the time.

"Nevertheless, whatever you saw is still in your memory banks," he added. "I would like the opportunity to retrieve that memory through hypnosis."

"You mean, like, put me into a trance?"

"Precisely! You can tell all your friends afterwards. It will be the most exciting thing that has ever happened to you."

"I don't know, Professor. I've had enough excitement lately. And that trance thing sounds kinda spooky."

"Don't you trust me, Justin?"

"Of course I do, Professor! You got me that lawyer. Oh, okay, I'll do it. Hey, wait a minute! Can you fix it so I quit smoking while you're at it?"

McCabe promised to try, although he admitted that he had never given anyone a post-hypnotic suggestion to break the smoking habit. He warned that more than one session might be necessary to achieve success.

"First, however, I will want to ask you those questions," he said.

"Okay, let's get it on," Bird said. "You gonna dangle a watch in front of me, or a coin, or what?"

"I prefer to use a candle in the dark," McCabe said. "It wouldn't work for a stage performance, but here it will be perfect."

He closed the blinds on the windows and turned down the lights. He pulled a candle out of his

sport coat pocket and lit it. It was about six inches long
and the diameter of a dime.

"Now, Justin," he said in a soothing voice, "the
darkness will close in on the light. I want you to focus
on the light. Listen only to my voice and to my words.
You are relaxed, totally relaxed, and getting more
relaxed. The darkness is closing in. You are getting
drowsy. The sound of my voice is lulling you to sleep . .
. a wonderful, welcome sleep. Your eyelids are getting
heavy, so heavy you can no longer keep them from
closing." This went on for several minutes. "You are
now in a deep sleep, Justin. Do you understand?"

"Yes."

"This is the evening of Thursday, May 10. You
are excited because it is the opening night of the play,
1895."

"Yes, the play. I helped!" Bird's words were
distinct and yet his voice seemed to be coming from a
distance.

"You helped a lot, Justin. In fact, you are
helping now. The play has been going on and you are
backstage. Look around you. What do you see?"

"It's a mess. There's scenery and props and all
kinds of junk everywhere. And lots of people."

"What people? Who do you see?"

"There's Professor McCabe and Mr. Figg.
They're arguing again. Why can't they just get along?"

"Who else?"

"There's Dr. LaBelle—I like that rose tattoo on
her leg. She's awful pretty. I wouldn't mind looking at
her for a while. But I have to pay attention in case Sister
Polly needs me to help her fix something. So I'm
standing right by her. She's nice. She listens to me."
Bird assumed a pouty expression. "I don't care what my
mother says, I think those Catholics are okay."

"We try, Justin. But you can't stand by Sister Polly the whole time, can you? You have a certain craving."

"A cigarette! Yeah, I need a cigarette real bad."

"So what do you do about that?"

"I go outside. Can't let Sister Polly see me. I told her I quit and I don't want to disappoint her. She always looks real sad when I disappoint her."

"How do you get outside?"

"There's a back door, toward the left. I hope Sister Polly won't notice if I mosey my way back there. Once I get close to the door nobody will see me because that's behind the scenery."

"So whatever's going on back there, only you will see. What do you see?"

"Nothin'."

McCabe frowned. "There's nobody there?"

"Just Mrs. Hudson standing at the other end of the room."

"Mrs. Hudson!"

"That's just her name in the play. She's really Mrs. Apple. She's talking on a cell phone and looking out the window at the back."

McCabe lifted one eyebrow. "Do you hear anything?"

"No, I—Oh, yeah. There was a noise, a funny little pop, right before she closed the cell phone. It was outside the theater, but close."

"What does Mrs. Apple do after she closes the cell phone?"

"She starts walking toward the front end of the backstage area, where all the people are."

"What do you do?"

"I'm walking out to get my smoke. Wait a minute! Something's wrong. Somebody's lying on the ground. He must be drunk."

"He's not drunk, Justin," McCabe said grimly. "Now I want to take you back to Sunday evening, when you were hit by the car . . ."

Chapter Thirty-Three
Treasure Hunt

By pre-arrangement via text-message, I met Lynda and Triple M at Beans & Books for cappuccino after their taekwondo class. The coffee house and bookstore does a brisk evening business, thanks to its liquor license and hip atmosphere. Starbucks across the street is okay for a quick cup, but Beans & Books has the ambience.

Both women were happily exhausted from their workout. With Justin Bird no longer under suspicion and out of the coma, Triple M was looking rested and cheerful. Her black, chin-length hair was shiny and her eyes bright.

"It's been an interesting day," I said. "We spent a good part of it in Louisville. I brought you a little something."

I handed over the fifth of Old Ben, carefully pointing out the signature on the bottle. "Mac and I spent about an hour talking to him."

"That's just awesome!" Lynda said. Maybe I should have waited until we were alone to present this special gift. She certainly looked appreciative. "That man is a living legend in the industry. The cover story about him in *Bourbon Review* last year called him 'Citizen Cain.'"

"He's offering a reward or finder's fee of twenty percent—fifty thousand dollars—to anybody who can recover his ransom money," I said.

From there I had to backfill with what we'd learned about Kirtland's involvement in the Bart Cain kidnapping.

"But Mac doesn't think the kidnappers killed him?" Triple M asked. Although practically floating that Justin was no longer under the cloud of suspicion or the threat of death, she was still interested in justice for her old boyfriend.

"He's got this idea that Justin must know something subconsciously, or the murderer thinks he does, and that's the reason for the hit-and-run. He's talking to Justin now—under hypnosis."

"Hypnosis!" Lynda and Triple M said in chorus.

I shrugged, as if to say, "That's Mac!"

"I've been thinking about the ransom money," I said. "If the kidnappers don't have it, and they didn't kill Bill Kirtland, then either the killer has it or he hasn't been able to find it yet."

"You have a keen perception of the obvious, Jeff," said my beloved, not for the first time. "What you're saying is, it has to be somewhere."

Clearly my genius was not being appreciated.

"Actually, if the killer doesn't have it, there are only two likely places—Bill's car and Shamrocks & Ivy. Bill didn't go anywhere else where he could have hidden it. We've got most of his day covered and nobody saw him hauling around anything with him that could have contained a quarter of a million bucks."

"Okay, so maybe it's in his car and his sister will find it," Triple M said.

"Or maybe it's at the B&B and we'll find it." I countered.

"You mean in his room?" Lynda said.

I shook my head. "No, I'm sure that's been cleaned out by now. Mary Rose Kirtland took Bill's effects, and I'm sure the Apples have the room ready for the next guest. There might be someplace he could hide it in the parlor or dining room, but I'm thinking the basement would be more likely. I think we should go back to Shamrocks & Ivy right now and give it a look."

Triple M yawned. "Well, have fun, kiddies. And give me a call if you find the ransom."

"You're not going?" Lynda said.

"I'm tired. Besides, three's a crowd." She wiggled her eyebrows suggestively. If I'd done that, Lynda would have kicked me under the table. There is no justice in this world.

"Okay." Lynda stood up. "Let's give this a whirl. It'll be like a treasure hunt."

If you ever go on a treasure hunt, take my advice: Make sure the pirates are gone first.

We walked down the rickety steps to the basement with me in the lead.

"On second thought," Lynda said behind me, "those kids on *Scooby-Doo* always get into big trouble when they do something like this."

I should have paid attention, but noooo, I said, "Ha! We're not kids. We're seasoned investigators."

The basement had whitewashed stone walls and a concrete floor. Here and there were boxes. An old ping-pong table was shoved up against one wall and a refrigerator stood in a corner.

"Let's start with the boxes," I suggested, kneeling down and opening one.

"All right."

After about ten minutes of frantic box-opening, we had ample evidence that the Apples were very big on Christmas decorating. So far my brainstorm was raining on my own parade.

I stood up and looked around.

"I was hoping for a cellar with some nicely aged fine wines," I joked.

"They've got the cobwebs for it."

"Not everywhere," I observed. "There aren't any on that old refrigerator over there. I'd say it's been in use. Let's give it a look."

"Sure." I could almost read her mind: *I'll humor him now, but after we're married . . .*

I opened the door of the refrigerator. It was filled with stacks of money. Stacks and stacks. Filled. I blinked but they didn't go away. I opened my mouth but nothing came out. I just stared at Lynda, who stared back at me, having already stared at the money.

"I guess this is what they mean by cold cash," I said finally.

"You know, that was actually brilliant," Lynda said. "I mean, figuring out to look down here and then coming up with that that whole no-cobwebs thing was just Sherlock Holmes smart. That out-McCabes McCabe, darling." She gave me a quick, girlish kiss.

Just as I started to bask in this adoration from my sweetheart, hoping that she would gaze adoringly into my eyes for a while longer, my smart phone plinked. I hauled it out of my pocket and looked at a text from Mac as Lynda read over my shoulder: *Avoid B&B. Apples are the killers.*

"Oh, shit," Lynda said. "Maybe you were too smart." Talk about bad timing, Mac. *Too late*, I responded. *We're here. Found the money!*

Just as I grabbed Lynda's hand, ready to bolt out of there and to hell with the money, I heard the stairs creak. We froze in place and watched as a pair of legs descended. Eventually George Apple's face with his white goatee came into view. Never had Col. Sanders looked so menacing. He had his hands in his pockets.

"Evening, folks."

If he didn't know that we knew, maybe we could bluff our way out of this.

"Whew," I said. "We heard a noise, like maybe a burglar." I was hoping he would put down the trembling in my voice to the lingering effects of a scare. "Good thing it's you."

"I don't think so," he said. "Not from your point of view."

He withdrew his right hand, and a gun with it.

"Is that the gun you used to kill Bill Kirtland with?" Lynda asked. *So much for playing dumb!*

George looked offended. "What kind fool do you take me for, Missy? I threw Kirtland's gun down a storm drain, along with the half-gallon milk bottle I used to muffle the noise."

A milk bottle! "Is that why Sally complained the day after the murder about you not buying a new one?"

"Hey, you're pretty slick, Jeff! Yep, that's why. Anyway, this is a new gun. I bought it after the murder to defend my home since Erin has become such a dangerous place. I had no idea, of course, that I was going to have to use it against one of my own guests. You were trying to rob me, see, and when I caught you, you attacked me and I had to shoot you to defend myself. I don't think there'll be much of a problem."

"Why did you do it?" Lynda asked. "Kill Bill, I mean." *Good girl. Keep him talking. Talking is better, much better, than shooting.*

"I had a suitcase full of reasons, missy. That's where Kirtland had the money—in a big blue suitcase in his room."

"But how did you know that?" I was assuming the suitcase wasn't sitting open, showing the greenbacks.

George actually looked embarrassed. "Times are tough, in case you haven't noticed. As a business, Shamrocks & Ivy just isn't making it. We're close to foreclosure. So we've been dipping into the guests' luggage and drawers here and there, things we could sell easily but might not be missed for a while. It's a living, you know? When we saw all that cash, we just couldn't believe it. It was like an answer to a prayer. There was enough to get us through these lean times, and then some. We wouldn't have to default on the mortgage."

"So you decided to take the money," I said. "But this was no petty thievery that would go unnoticed, so you figured you had to kill Bill Kirtland to cover the theft." George nodded. "You were really pretty clever about it, if I have this right." *Play to his ego. He won't kill you as long as you make him feel superior. Maybe.* "You didn't want to take the money away in the suitcase because somebody might be able to trace it back to Kirtland. So you took the dough and hid it where you figured nobody would ever look. Then you stole his backup gun from his room and used it to kill him because you knew it would never be traced to you."

This is where he was supposed to say, "And I would have gotten away with it, too, if it hadn't been for you meddlesome kids." Had the man never seen *Scooby-Doo?* Oh, wait. He *was* going to get away with it.

No, that's not what I was thinking at the time. I was looking for a way out and not seeing it. At least Lynda and I would die together, but that was small comfort. We would still die. I hoped she would forgive me for getting her into this mess.

"Okay, so you hid the money away after Bill left for the theater that night," Lynda said. "Why didn't you just wait for him to come back here to kill him? That would have been a lot less risky than doing it out in public."

George gave an "I'm-smarter-than-you" smile. "The streets of downtown Erin on a week night are not very public. If we'd killed him here, we would have had to move his body somewhere else so that the murder wouldn't be connected with Shamrocks & Ivy and its genial owners. I think that would have been riskier."

"But now you're going to shoot us in your basement," I said.

The man with the gun shook his head. "No, I'm going to shoot you in our bedroom. That would be much more realistic. Remember, you were trying to rob us and I caught you at it. You aimed a gun at me, so I had to defend myself."

"But we're unarmed!" Lynda exclaimed.

"You won't be. We've got another gun. Always have a backup. Now let's go upstairs."

"Why the hell should we do that? You're going to shoot us anyway."

"Because every moment you live is a moment you live. And there's always the hope that I'll have a heart attack climbing the stairs."

Hey, that's not so far-fetched for an overweight senior citizen. Is it a sin to pray for that?

George waved us in front of him with his gun. I motioned for Lynda to go up the stairs first.

As we mounted the creaky stairs, I tried hard to work up the courage to fall backward onto George. The gun might go off in my back, but at least I would knock George backward down the stairs and give Lynda a chance to run like hell. It was really a very good plan except that (A) George lagged too far behind me, and (B) I probably didn't have the nerve anyway.

When Lynda reached the top of the stairs, George yelled for her to stop on the landing, then told me to join her. Once he caught up with us he directed us forward. But Lynda stopped in the kitchen.

"Could I have a cigarette?"

I guess this is no time to say I was proud of you for quitting and you really shouldn't let the pressure get to you.

"Sorry, Missy," George said. "It just wouldn't be smart for me to let you—"

I think he was going to say something like "go into your purse," but he didn't have a chance. While he was still talking, Lynda moved forward into his personal space. What followed happened so fast it didn't all quite register on the Cody mind. Lynda told me later that she grabbed George's gun-holding hand by the wrist while pulling his arm straight out and to the side of her. Then she smashed upward with her fist into his elbow, breaking the elbow and his ulna. Before he dropped the gun in pain he managed to get off one wild shot. *BOOM!* I almost crapped my pants right there. The bullet went through an overhead light, breaking a bulb, and into the ceiling. George was down, and he wasn't moving.

"What the hell was that?!" I said.

"Taekwondo, of course." Lynda was breathing hard, provoking incongruously amorous emotions in her fiancé. My heart was racing, and not just from the excitement of our near-death experience.

"Don't move."

I moved, of course. I had to turn around. It was Sally Apple, looking considerably less like the Pillsbury Doughboy with a gun in her hand. *Oh, yeah. I'd forgotten about her.*

"You'd better hope he's not dead, or you'll die slowly rather than quickly," she said.

All of a sudden, there was a big cracking noise and the back door flew open. Was I hallucinating, or was that Jake Teal standing there aiming his service gun—sorry, firearm—at Sally Apple?

"Daddy!" Lynda cried.

"Mac called me," her father drawled. "He seemed to think you might need some help."

Chapter Thirty-Four
Confessions of a Contrite Sleuth

"I was at the hospital and I knew that Jake, if he were at the apartment or—*ahem*—at our house, could get to Shamrocks & Ivy faster than I could," Mac said.

We were sipping Lynda's homemade limoncello after dinner at Mac's the next day. Lynda's parents were with us, and Triple M, but the McCabe children had cleared out after dessert. Brian was probably beating Rebecca at chess as usual (needing no help from Uncle Jeff) and Amanda, the middle child, was studying for a history test in abject fear that her grade point average might slip below 99.

"What exactly did Justin tell you?" Triple M asked Mac. Her young charge was still at St. Hildegard. Now George Apple was there, too, under guard while recovering from the broken wrist, broken ulna, and other injuries inflicted on him by my favorite taekwondo black belt. Both were expected to be released from the hospital in the next day or two—to jail, in George's case.

"He saw Sally Apple looking out the window while she was talking on her cell phone. After he heard a popping noise—Kirtland's gunshot through the makeshift silencer—she closed her phone. Connecting the dots was not difficult. Sally must have called Kirtland earlier on the throwaway cell phone with some story that got his attention. Perhaps she started to tell him something that sounded important, then said she had to go but he should keep his cell phone on vibrate because she would call again. I am sure she was convincing. She has some small talent as an actress. Then she called back during the performance and asked him to leave the theater. Watching him out the window, she told him exactly where to stand so that her husband would have a clear shot. The call was both a lure and a distraction. Concentrating on the phone call, his senses would have been less attuned to any sounds that George Apple made while approaching him from behind."

"Talk about cold blood," I murmured.

"My little experiment in hypnosis proved so successful that I also asked Justin to remember who was behind the wheel of the car that ran over him. He didn't know George Apple, but I recognized the description from the one time Apple picked up his wife after a rehearsal. That is when I texted you, Jeff. By thunder, it never should have gotten that far. I was a dolt. There were so many clues I should have figured it out even without Justin's testimony. You even gave me one, Jake."

Lynda's father looked startled. "I did?"

His ex-wife, stunningly arrayed in a black cocktail dress with a plunging neckline and diamond earrings, looked adoringly at him.

"You said the part you liked about *1895* was that the murderer was close to home. What could be closer to home for Bill Kirtland while he was in Erin than the bed and breakfast at which he was staying? Later, Ben Cain described the blue suitcase in which he put the ransom money. One of the two suitcases in Kirtland's room matched that description perfectly. Ergo, the suitcase never left his room. However, his sister never mentioned finding a quarter of a million dollars in it. There was no reason for her not to, if it had been there—she would have assumed that it was her money as Kirtland's heir. If the suitcase with the ransom money never left the house, then perhaps the money did not either—and that pointed to the Apples."

"You're being too hard on yourself," I said. Yes, I really said that. I still can't believe I would ever have occasion to utter those words, but I thought Mac was missing something. "You couldn't really know that the suitcase was empty," I pointed out. "Mary Rose Kirtland is a single mom whose ex-husband is a deadbeat dad. Suppose she found a suitcase full of money, origin unknown. Unless she's that honest person Diogenes has been looking for all these years, it wouldn't be too surprising if she forgot to mention it to anybody—no inheritance taxes, no police investigation of where the money came from.

"Beside, you never saw the suitcase, Mac."

"Yes, I did, Jefferson. One of those photos of the room that you e-mailed me had a clear shot of the suitcase. I saw, but I did not observe." He was kind enough not to mention that I saw that suitcase in person and it didn't register on me, not even after Ben Cain referred to his suitcase as "Big Blue."

"As for Mary Rose Kirtland," Mac added, "I suppose you do have a point, as a theoretical proposition."

"I still find it hard to believe that anybody would just leave two hundred and fifty thousand dollars sitting around in a rented room," Lynda said, "much less a private investigator."

"He didn't know he was checking into the Bates Motel," Triple M said, as if defending her late friend.

"I've never had anything stolen from me in a hotel, motel, or bed and breakfast," Jake mused. "And I've been in a lot of them all over the world."

"I'd bet that he had his room and suitcase both locked, and the suitcase probably hidden away," I said. "But George was apparently good with locks. He admitted stealing from guests before. I'm sure he stole a nice pair of earrings from Amy Quong, but then snuck them back when she noticed they were missing. By that time, with the ransom money sitting in their basement refrigerator, the value of the earrings was chickenfeed."

"The theft of Bill Kirtland's backup gun also should have pointed me in the direction of George and Sally Apple," Mac said. "Their B&B was the most likely place for it to have been taken from. It certainly was not stolen from his person on

Thursday night and then used to kill him. No, he left it behind in his room on an evening when he had no reason to believe he would be facing danger."

Triple M sipped her third glass of limoncello, not that I was counting. "Poor Justin! I guess he's going to be okay—"

"Better than okay!" Mac said. "I gave him a post-hypnotic suggestion to quit smoking. Let me know if he starts to weaken and I'll give him a booster."

"—but I still feel bad for him that he almost got killed just for being in the wrong place at the wrong time."

"Maybe that was my fault." Everybody looked at me. Did I ever mention that Lynda has beautiful brown eyes, not as wide as her mother's, but flecked with gold? Well, she does.

"As I look back, it seems obvious to me now that George was constantly pumping me for information about the case. He knew we're close to Oscar and also that we were asking a few questions on our own to help Justin. He and Sally probably didn't worry about Justin seeing anything at first, but when I raised that possibility they must have gotten nervous. Even if he didn't remember anything now, something might occur to him later. So he had to go. George told me he used to repossess cars for a living, so maybe that's where he picked up his skills in hot-wiring."

Lucia shuddered theatrically, which was quite a performance if you were looking at it, which I was. "That awful woman, his wife! I cannot believe she almost killed my precious Lynda!"

Her precious Lynda gave me one of her patented eye-rolls, which in this case I interpreted to mean "puh-lease."

"I fear that it would not have been the first time—or should I say, the second," Mac said. "Oscar tells me that her first husband was killed in Ann Arbor eleven years ago— supposedly during a robbery while Sally was away. The police suspected the robbery was ersatz, but they could never prove anything. Six months later Sally married George Apple. They'd been seen together while her husband was still alive."

It's amazing the things that people do for love and money, even senior citizens who look like Col. Sanders and the Pillsbury Doughgirl.

"How do you execute people here in Ohio?" Jake asked.

"Lethal injection," Mac said. "However, the charge against Sally at this point is only accessory to murder. And Erica Slade has already signed on to defend her. My sources"— probably Erica herself—"tell me that Ms. Slade will argue that Sally was the victim of a modified form of Stockholm Syndrome, whereby victims come to identify with their captors. She will claim that George was the real villain and Sally was so emotionally bonded to him that she could not resist his will."

"That defense didn't work too well for Patty Hearst, as I recall," Jake said. "She did time."

Mac shrugged. "It will be entertaining, if nothing else— Erica squaring off against her ex-husband in court. She has a better chance than the public defender handling George's case."

"Speaking of captors," Kate said, "at least the one good thing out of all of this is that the little boy, Bart Cain, is back with his parents. He may never remember his ordeal. And Ben Cain has his money back—I'm sure he's very grateful for that!"

I grinned. "Very grateful indeed." *Twenty percent of the ransom grateful.*

Chapter Thirty-Five
"All the Days of My Life"

Ben Cain even threw in a case of Old Ben, the single barrel, 120-proof variety, along with the financial reward. Lynda got all of the bourbon, but we agreed to split the reward fifty-fifty. Most of the time that wouldn't matter; we had decided to commingle our funds instead of keeping separate accounts. But Lynda wanted to use her share to help Mary Rose Kirtland's kids. I was all for that, but I invested my half in stock and bond index funds. Somebody has to save for our future children's educations.

1895 was performed one more weekend, this time without Sally Apple. There was no time for an audition to replace her, and there was no understudy, so Mac pressed Kate into service as possibly the tallest and youngest Mrs. Hudson ever to trod the boards. Lynda and I saw the play again—all the way through this time—and we thought Kate did quite well. Art in the blood is liable to take the strangest forms, as somebody once said.

The play completed its run, St. Benignus held commencement, and the following weekend Lynda and I promised before God and two hundred people to be true to each other in good times and bad, in sickness and in health, and to love and honor each other "all the days of my life."

By the wedding day, May 26, Mac's beard was already growing back. I have to admit he cut quite an impressive figure as the best man in his traditional tuxedo, black with a black bow tie. This time I was wearing a bow tie myself.

A half-hour or so before the march down the aisle, I stood at the back of the church, feeling strangely calm in the midst of chaos. Then the front doors opened on a sight that took my breath away. It was a handsome woman in her early sixties, strawberry hair fading to gray, being wheeled in.

"Mom!" I gasped.

My father, standing behind her wheelchair, peered at me through his owlish T.S. Eliot glasses. "I couldn't hold her back, Jeff."

"I hear there's a party tonight," she said. "You know I never miss a good party." My mother, slightly more introverted than the Sphinx, hates parties.

Blinking back the waterworks, I bent down to kiss her.

And I thought I'd been happy before.

Before I knew it, it was 6:30. *Show time!*

Lynda looked radiant, of course, with her curly, honey blond hair in a French twist providing a clear view of her mother's diamond earrings. The wedding dress she made was perfect, but I bet most of the guests were looking at who walked her down the aisle when *Jesu, Joy of Man's Desiring* started coming out of the organ. Lynda had one parent on each arm, and they were the handsomest couple ever seen this far east of Hollywood. Lucia, incredibly, wore a flowing scarlet dress that—although elegant—was quite suitable for church, and Jake's tux looked like it was tailored made to fit him. They presented their daughter to me with a hug (Lucia) and a handshake (Jake). "Over to you, Jeff," the Colonel whispered.

Lynda's bridesmaid sister, Emma Teal, was as gorgeous in person as in her photo. But she seemed awfully young. Oscar Hummel, her partner for the ceremony, looked about as comfortable in a tuxedo as a gorilla in a white tie and tails. Apparently Triple M does wear earrings, at least at weddings where she is the maid of honor, and the gold loops looked great with her dark blue dress.

Before we pronounced our vows, Fr. Peter Nguyen gave a memorable homily. Everybody says so. But I don't remember it. What sticks in my mind most about that evening is not the words but a few images, clearer in my recollection than any wedding photo. From the wedding Mass, it's Lynda walking down the aisle between her parents, her lovely oval face split with a radiant smile. From the reception in the ballroom of Winfield Hotel, it's Lynda dancing with her father to Frank Sinatra singing "The Way You Look Tonight."

In my own turn around the dance floor with Lynda, I held my bride close, closed my eyes, and breathed in the intoxicating smell of Cleopatra VII perfume.

"*Ti voglio bene, tesoro mio,*" her husky voice came in my right ear. "What are you thinking?"

I opened my eyes and looked around the dance floor at all the familiar faces that had meant so much to me—my parents, Kate, Oscar, Popcorn, Fr. Pirelli, the tiresome Ralph Pendergast, his surprisingly attractive wife, Triple M, and—magically producing a white rose out of thin air for Lucia—the one and only Sebastian McCabe. Something the Colonel had once said came back to me.

"I think we're going to live an interesting life together," I said. "In fact, I'm absolutely sure of it."

A FEW WORDS OF THANKS

Thomas Jefferson Cody, who is currently exhausted from his honeymoon and the events that followed (but that's another book), joins me in expressing our debt and our gratitude to the following family members, friends, and experts whose contributions to the preparation of this manuscript for publication were invaluable:

Ann Brauer Andriacco, for her constant support;

Daniel, Michael, and Elizabeth Andriacco, and their spouses, for their tolerance;

Tony Andriacco, my brother, for a great job of proofreading and cheerleading;

Felicia Carparelli, for helpful suggestions in the early going;

Sr. Eileen Connelly, Tricia Hempel, and Kieran McMullen for technical advice on (respectively) women religious Army veterans, taekwondo, and guns;

Jeff Suess, for proofreading and final preparation of the manuscript.

Whatever errors remain in this book are solely the responsibility of the author and his literary agent.

Once again I thank Steve Emecz for being my publisher and Bob Gibson at Stauch Design for producing yet another outstanding cover.

Special thanks go to Matt Laffey of the always interesting always1895.net blog. I strongly suspect that the inspiration for Sebastian McCabe's *1895* play came from Matt, and I know for certain that the bumper sticker mentioned on page 11 did.

Dan Andriacco
August 2012

About the Author

Dan Andriacco has been reading mysteries since he discovered Sherlock Holmes at the age of nine, and writing them almost as long. The first two books in his popular Sebastian McCabe – Jeff Cody series are *No Police Like Holmes* and *Holmes Sweet Holmes.*

A member of the Tankerville Club, a scion society of The Baker Street Irregulars, since 1981, he is also the author of *Baker Street Beat: An Eclectic Collection of Sherlockian Scribblings.* Follow his blog at www.danandriacco.com, his tweets at *@DanAndriacco,* and his Facebook Fan Page at www.facebook.com/DanAndriaccoMysteries.

Dr. Dan and his wife, Ann, have three grown children and four grandchildren. They live in Cincinnati, Ohio, USA, about forty miles downriver from Erin.

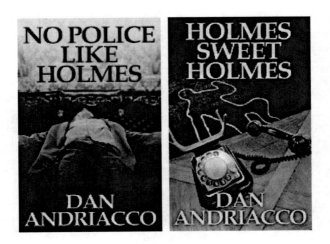

Sebastian McCabe, Jeff Cody, and Lynda Teal will return in
The Disappearance of Mr. James Phillimore

Also from MX Publishing

  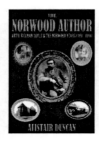 

Four books on Sir Arthur Conan Doyle by Alistair Duncan including a an overview of all the stories (**Eliminate The Impossible**), a London guide (**Close to Holmes**), the winner of the Howlett Award 2011 (**The Norwood Author**) and the book on Undershaw (**An Entirely New Country**).

Short fiction collections from Tony Reynolds (**Lost Stories of Sherlock Holmes**), Gerard Kelly (**The Outstanding Mysteries of Sherlock Holmes**) and Bertram Fletcher Robinson (**Aside Arthur Conan Doyle**).

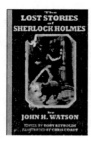 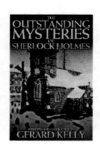 

www.mxpublishing.com

Also From MX Publishing

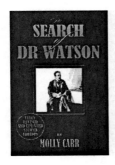  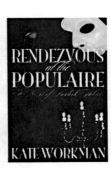

A biography **(In Search of Dr Watson)**, a travel guide **(Sherlock Holmes and Devon)**, a novel where Sherlock Holmes battles The Phantom **(Rendezvous at The Populaire)**, a novel featuring Dr.Watson **(Watson's Afghan Adventure)**, a fantasy novel **(Shadowfall)** and an intriguing collection of papers from The Hound **(The Official Papers Into The Matter Known as The Hound of The Baskervilles)**.

www.mxpublishing.com

Also From MX Publishing

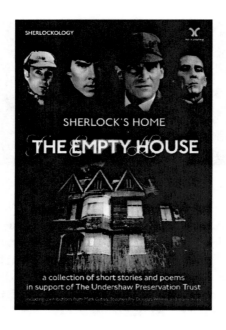

More than 40 stories and contributions from Holmes writers
worldwide including Stephen Fry, Mark Gatiss, Nick Briggs and
Douglas Wilmer.

Raising awareness for the campaign to preserve Sir Arthur
Conan Doyle's home. All the royalties from the book go to the
trust.

www.saveundershaw.com

Also From MX Publishing

A complete review of all the 56 short stories and the four
novels in the Sherlock Holmes canon.

Taken from the astonishing blog Charlotte Walters wrote in the
lead up to the launch of her debut novel Barefoot on Baker
Street. Charlotte reviewed the 56 short stories one a day for 56
days in a row.

All the royalties from the book go to the Undershaw
Preservation Trust.

www.facebook.com/saveundershaw